I0819584

CABARET IN FLAMES

BY HACHE PUEYO

But Not Too Bold

AS H. PUEYO

A Study in Ugliness & Outras Histórias

CABARET IN FLAMES

HACHE PUEYO

TOR PUBLISHING GROUP

NEW YORK

This is a work of fiction. All of the names, characters, organizations, places, and events portrayed in this work are either products of the author's imagination or used fictitiously.

CABARET IN FLAMES

A Tordotcom Book
Published by Tom Doherty Associates / Tor Publishing Group
120 Broadway
New York, NY 10271

www.torpublishinggroup.com

EU Representative: Macmillan Publishers Ireland Ltd, 1st Floor, The Liffey Trust Centre, 117–126 Sheriff Street Upper, Dublin 1, D01 YC43

The Library of Congress Cataloging-in-Publication Data
is available upon request.

ISBN 978-1-250-37045-7 (hardcover)
ISBN 978-1-250-37046-4 (ebook)

First Edition: 2026

Printed in the United States of America

10 9 8 7 6 5 4 3 2 1

CABARET IN FLAMES

I

Ariadne's Thread

Fireworks crackled outside when he appeared at her door. The neighbors set them off during football matches and to show whether or not they agreed with the news, but the noise that night was louder, thundering above the buildings like lost bullets. The visitor introduced himself as Quaint, no surname, following the tradition of his kind. *My sobriquet since the nineteenth century,* he would later say, *coined by my late wife.*

In age, Quaint looked like he could be anywhere in that nebulous period of adult life that ranged from thirty to fifty, but it was more, much more.

"Hello, gul doctor," he said through the speaker of the intercom. Only his lower jaw and a fragment of his black umbrella appeared on the screen. "It's been a long time."

Ariadne never allowed anyone in her house after curfew, let alone a man, but something in his words made her press the button that unlocked the front door. Perhaps it had been the certainty with which Quaint had spoken, hinting at an intimacy they did not share, or perhaps she was intrigued by the fact that he was a healthy adult male. Most of her patients were elderly, disabled, or pregnant, harmless save for a few exceptions, so his presence in the clinic sparked her curiosity, making her wonder what a mature gul could want with her.

After climbing the last step, Quaint stood in the stairwell, just the silhouette of a tall man in the penumbra. It was like seeing a panther lurking in the darkness, well-built and alluring, waiting until the prey would walk into the trap.

"Are you Miss Yurkova, I wonder?" Quaint shook the umbrella, sprinkling water on the floor. His words echoed through the corridor, sending an unpleasant chill down every vertebra of her spine: *wonder, wonder, wonder.*

Ariadne frowned, staring at the metallic sign on the door that announced ERIK YURKOV, MD right under number 201.

"In a way, yes."

"Erik, living with another person? That's an achievement I didn't expect of him." He stepped forward and his shadow stretched from the stairs to the door of her apartment. "Are you his girlfriend? Daughter, perhaps?"

Ariadne moved aside to let him in. *We're nothing anymore,* she thought, but her mouth answered:

"Apprentice."

"Oh! Another gul doctor?"

Under the light, Quaint became somebody else: black hair slicked back with an undercut, golden-ocher skin, a long flat nose, and a pair of round sunglasses that hid his expression, but still she felt his eyes on her, analyzing every hint of movement. He wore a mustard-yellow shirt, suspenders, black pants, and there were raindrops on the leather of his shoes. What surprised Ariadne most, however, were not his fine clothes or the heavy rings covering his fingers, but the tattoos on his hands, neck, and the part of his chest exposed by the open collar.

Ariadne bristled like a cornered cat. "Are you human?"

"I'm fascinated by this question." Quaint smiled, and the tips of his canines appeared between his lips. Adult guls could have as many as eleven pairs of sharp fangs, mirroring human premolars and cuspids, and every additional tooth increased their bite force.

"I've never seen a tattooed gul before. How . . . ?"

Ariadne glanced at the sideboard. Inside the drawer was a dose of carfentanil strong enough to take down an elephant. Quaint was twice her size and she should have never been alone with him, but one shot of the tranquilizer and he would be as inoffensive as a child. It was not necessary; after a moment of silence, Quaint began to laugh.

"A strange sight, I've been told," said Quaint, still smiling, one of his hands covering his teeth. She flinched with the gesture. "That's one of the reasons I'm here, in fact. My tattoos have been fading faster than normal."

"What are you, a masochist?"

"Far from it, but Erik will know what to do. Can you call him, Miss . . . ?"

Erik again. Everything always went back to Erik in the end.

"Ariadne. And no, I can't."

Another firecracker exploded outside, followed by whistles and howls. The neighbor's dog, from one of the houses across the street, barked at the sound, and other dogs followed suit.

"See, Miss Ariadne, I know I should have announced my arrival, and that you have quite the temper," stated Quaint, raising two smoky eyebrows, "but Erik and I have been friends for many lives. I need to talk to him. Tell him it's to rest my heart. I've had the most unsettling dream."

"First, *Mister* Quaint . . ." Ariadne answered calmly. Her legs throbbed, and the stumps of her thighs felt sore against the prosthesis after a long day of work. "You know nothing of my temper. Second, I can't call Erik because he's no longer here. Or anywhere—might be dead, for all I know."

Quaint opened his mouth to reply, but he gave up before even starting. His shoulders slumped, a thick wrinkle appeared in his forehead, and he touched the ring on his little finger.

"So Erik is really gone."

"He's not *gone*, Mister Quaint. He just left. Vanished five years ago and never told me why."

"Only Quaint, please."

"I'm guessing you're not from here based on your name, your clothes, and the fact that I've never seen you before, despite your claiming to be his friend . . ."

"And you're right. I did live in Brazil in the past, but moved back home in 2009. Time . . ."

". . . passes differently for guls. *I know.* Well, I regret being the bearer of bad news, but you won't find anything of Erik here." Ariadne touched the key chain hanging from the door. "Do you want me to help you or will only Erik do?"

Quaint grinned, but the energy of his previous laughter was gone.

"Ha! Now I understand why Erik chose you as an apprentice. You're bold enough for the two of you." His hands slipped inside the pockets of his pants, and he straightened his posture. "Forgive the verbiage, I wasn't expecting such news."

"Please follow me."

"In a second."

Years later, Ariadne would still wonder if Quaint knew he would come into her house to stay, since he always seemed to know more than others around him. If he did, he never told her, and he acted as sincerely as she had then. He followed her into the consultation room and unbuttoned his shirt, revealing an already faded chest piece towering over the images that covered the rest of his torso. The central tattoo depicted two birds, one on each shoulder, their spread wings meeting at his sternum. The black ink had turned blue, unlike the guardian lion on his neck, fresh and recently remade.

"The problem lies in your regeneration speed." Ariadne's gloved finger brushed against the tattoo on his inner arm, a branch of guaraná, its fruits looking like insistent wide eyes. "But I would have to investigate why it changed out of nowhere."

"Thank you, Ariadne. Please accept my apologies for appearing so late at night." Quaint offered a discreet bow of the head, and unlocked his phone to input her number. A scream outside interrupted their conversation, but Ariadne just shook her head, telling him to ignore it. "I must say, however, that I'm afraid Erik might not have left of his own accord. I have known him since his youth, and he's never done that before."

Ariadne stiffened. "He packed his bags and walked out the front door."

"Still, we shouldn't . . ." Quaint took a good look at her, then smiled cryptically. "Never mind. I'll talk to a few friends, and we can discuss the matter again at our next appointment."

Rua da Encruzilhada was a residential cul-de-sac located in Vitória, Espírito Santo, and it had only a few small businesses. The first was a three-story building with a compounding pharmacy downstairs and a clinic above, with a pair of residents: Ariadne, who lived with her cat in the duplex that belonged to Erik, and Ms. Terebê, a tiny gul shriveled like a fig who had been born somewhere in South America, long before the European invasion. The last was the coffee shop around the corner, managed by Boniface, an Italian immigrant whose presence attracted a steady clientele of ancient patients to her clinic.

Their diet consisted of flesh, blood, and bones of humans like herself, but Ariadne felt safer with them around.

While she waited for Quaint's next visit, Ariadne checked Erik's old address book for the clinic, but there was no entry under the letter *Q*. Admittedly, they were supposed to be friends, not patient and doctor, but the little black book was one of the few personal possessions Erik had left behind. Years had passed since she had touched his things—she hated them, in fact, those lifeless proofs of his abandonment—but she wanted some clue that Quaint spoke the truth.

"Ms. Terebê," said Ariadne one night. They were watching the news together on the small television on the counter.

The compounding pharmacy was open twenty-four hours, as Terebê rarely slept, but she closed the doors at eight, keeping a small window open in case there was a customer, which rarely happened after the curfew started.

Ms. Terebê lifted a gray, almost-invisible eyebrow.

"Hmm?"

"Did Erik have friends?"

The little screen continued to report the evening news: *"An open letter was published this morning against the curfew, signed by more than two thousand artists, journalists, writers, and actors . . . Despite rumors of an illness, the president made a statement today, reaffirming that the curfew has lowered crime rates all over the country, but provided no proof of . . ."*

Ms. Terebê opened the minibar and took a blood bag from it. She had several stocked inside, her own personal blood bank inside the comfort of her house, along with bone broth and several plastic boxes containing pureed meat. According to Terebê, everything was provided by friends who worked at local hospitals and morgues, but Ariadne never tried to check the veracity of this claim, and never would.

"I have something for you, too." The elderly woman took another plastic bag from the minibar, but instead of blood, it was a packet of human food. "Let's eat."

Ariadne recognized the bear-shaped chocolate graham crackers from her childhood, but the memory was foggy; it reminded her of something happy, something like being praised after a tough day, but she couldn't recall why or when. *Close your eyes and open your mouth*, someone had said, and she had stuck her tongue out in response, feeling the graham cracker melt against it.

"I didn't know they still made these," commented Ariadne, and her eyes fell on the expiration date: September 1996. The red packet remained untouched in her lap, and she almost gave up on asking any other questions.

"It's been a while," Terebê said after some moments of silence, her eyes barely visible under the creases of aged brown skin. The top of her head had only a few strands of fine white hair, and her mouth had withered to a thin pout. "Since you last said his name."

Only outside of her head. Inside, Erik's name always lingered, a dictionary entry with many synonyms: teacher, savior, protector, friend, object of adoration, traitor. Ariadne straightened the packet, still with the faint memory of the graham crackers' taste, the kind of taste that, once, Erik would have fought to replace—*I can't stand seeing you in pain*, he would have said.

"I had no reason to talk about him before."

The old woman muted the television. On the screen, an adviser answered questions in front of the Civil House, his right hand held close to his chest, all fingers gone except the thumb. Every other secretary seemed to be missing a limb, nowadays. Ariadne clenched her jaw at the sight, refusing to look at it. She couldn't do it, not with a gul around.

"Erik was only friends with my kind," said Terebê while Ariadne emptied the blood bag into a porcelain cup for her. She made an appreciative sound, nodding emphatically. "Yes, yes, good."

"Anyone you might recall? A foreigner, perhaps?"

Terebê sipped from the white cup, leaving a dark red mustache over her toothless mouth. Like many guls her age, she had two pairs of molar fangs left, but the incisors were all gone. Ariadne gently wiped her lips with a napkin, and the little gul continued to drink.

"I remember a woman. Tall, short hair, loud. Spaniard or French. Something of the sort."

"What about a man?" insisted Ariadne.

"Then it's the freak with the tattoos." Ms. Terebê drank

all the blood eagerly and left the empty cup on the floor next to their feet. "Why do you ask?"

"He visited the clinic."

"Didn't he and Erik fight? It's been months since the last time I saw him." Terebê touched the popping veins of her own arm. "I haven't seen him since you were little, I'd say. Before Erik even brought you here."

"Years," corrected Ariadne. "Many, *many* years."

Ms. Terebê caressed the back of Ariadne's hand with affection.

"Years," she repeated with a smile. "I forget how quickly you people grow."

The old woman said that Boniface might remember him as well, and that was her last word on the subject. After the telenovela Terebê watched every night at nine, she would no longer hold any kind of conversation, and the next day she had forgotten all questions about Quaint.

On Sunday, Ariadne left in the early morning, when the street was deserted. A few stray cats ate the remains of an Eshu offering, tearing apart the red and black paper, and one of the candles rolled down the pavement. She knocked on the front window of the coffee shop, and the door opened on its own.

There were cracked glasses on the floor, and the tables had been flipped upside down. Ariadne knelt down to right one of the fallen chairs and noticed one of them had gouge marks, as if they had been chewed by a large animal.

"Mr. Boni? What happened here?"

If he were human, Boniface would have been around sixty, with his receding hairline, his thick mustache, and the carved lines in the olive canvas of his face, but he looked like a young adult when close to Ms. Terebê. He was on all fours, washing up spilled soda, and gestured irritably as he spoke:

"Oh, those, those—those *fascistas*, you know who I mean! The boys patrolling the streets at night . . . My blood's still boiling because of them."

Not only his, it seemed, as there were reddish-brown stains on some of the discarded rags.

"The death squads?"

"They think they own everything!" Boniface got up and threw a broken bottle into a trash bag. His Bolognese accent was more apparent, and there was a gash closing slowly on one of his hands. "They came here last night, talked to me like we are on the same side—I've left my home to avoid their kind, Christ—and made a mess out of my place, as you can see." Ariadne raised her eyebrows, and Boniface slapped his own stomach with a grin. "They're here now."

"I'm trying to treat your dental damage, yet you refuse to follow my liquid diet." Ariadne sighed. "But that's not why I'm here. Mr. Boni, do you recall any of Erik's friends?"

Boniface stopped sweeping the trash. "Erik's *friends*?"

"More specifically, a gul with tattoos?"

"Tattoos and glasses. A good-looking fella. Yes, I talked to him once. Had a loud argument with Erik in the clinic, you could hear them for miles." Boniface brushed his mustache with a finger. "Came here later and called a taxi to the airport. And that was it."

Further investigation proved to be even less fruitful, and Ariadne gave up on finding anything about Quaint; if it was important, he would come again. She treated a woman from Chile the following month, a middle-aged gul who was finally expecting after several miscarriages. A geriatric pregnancy, considering her age, but the future mother swore that this time she was feeling well.

It's always been hard for us to have children, she said while Ariadne performed an ultrasound. *But in the last two hundred years, the birth rates . . .*

When the woman left, an unknown number, code +86, tried to contact the clinic incessantly. At first, Ariadne thought of ignoring it; most of her patients appeared without warning, and the few calls she received were scams from prisons in São Paulo and Rio de Janeiro or relentless harassment from telemarketing agencies. The ringing continued from the first hours in the morning to late in the afternoon, and when she finally decided to take the call, she heard the same words as before:

"Hello, gul doctor."

Ariadne held her breath. "It's been a while, Quaint."

"Yes, I realized only now that I should have called a couple days after our meeting, not two months. If you'll forgive my insolence . . ." His voice was muffled by car horns on the other side of the line. "Can I invite myself to your home again today? It's about Erik."

As much as she wanted the subject to stay buried and forgotten, she felt compelled to accept.

"I'm free for the rest of the day."

Ariadne went straight to the bedroom to find another shirt. She had been wearing sweatpants—gray, loose, and as insipid as they could get—and a long-sleeved black shirt to hide the synthetic skin of her arms; with the pregnant patient, she hadn't cared, but knowing that Quaint was coming made her find an additional layer of clothes that made the volume of her breasts look a little smaller, as if that could protect her in any way.

It's about Erik, she thought, slapping her own cheeks to take the thought out of her head. Maybe something bad had happened. Maybe he really was dead. The mirror stared back at her: her thick lips, the dark circles around her narrow black eyes, her shaved head. *I need to know; after this, I won't think of him again.*

Quaint arrived at 4:20, wearing a dark green three-piece that made her feel underdressed inside her own house. Ariadne made a gesture for him to follow her to the living room, and they sat on the armchairs facing each other.

"I've been thinking about your tattoos," she started before he could tackle the unwanted subject. "If you insist on continuing to hurt yourself, we should try to add heavier metals to the ink. Mercury, lead, antimony, maybe arsenic."

Quaint crossed his legs, resting one hand on his knee. This one had a blooming peony tattooed on the back, its spread petals covering up to his wrist. There were inked dates scattered on his long fingers, but the memento mori rings made them unintelligible.

"Sure, let's do it," answered Quaint. The white Angora she had found roaming the street the year before rubbed against his legs, meowing, and Quaint bent down to scratch her ears. "What's her name?"

"She doesn't have one yet."

"Are you feeling well? You look upset."

"It's nothing."

"Let me guess," continued Quaint, and the cat jumped onto his lap like she'd known him for years. "Erik never mentioned me, right?"

"He didn't," Ariadne admitted.

"How typical. He didn't tell me about you either. Which

is too bad, as you inherited his clinic and I have the key to his storage. If anything happened . . ."

"Storage?" The word made her look up. Ariadne had been staring at his rings for the past minute: a skull and crossbones with rubies, another made of gold with braided hair inside a crystal enclosure, a thin ring painted with black enamel.

Quaint took a key from his breast pocket, twirling it around his index finger.

"The only copy. I never asked what he keeps there, and he never told me."

"And where's this storage supposed to be?"

"Why, in his office."

"There's nothing there."

Erik had taken everything. Only the empty furniture remained, wooden carcasses decaying in his abandoned office.

"Can I take a look?"

Ariadne responded with a shrug. They went to the second floor, and the cat trailed behind them. Quaint didn't scare her now as much as he had on the first day, but she tried to keep him in sight. He went straight to the last closed door, moving with confidence in the corridor, like someone who had been many times before in an apartment that was supposedly hers.

"Quaint," called Ariadne. "How did you meet Erik?"

"It's complicated."

The office smelled like an old wardrobe that had not been opened in years, and inside were the desk, the chair, the shelves, and a massive cabinet that had so many drawers, doors, and locks that it had taken Ariadne months to clean all of it after Erik disappeared.

"Complicated means you won't tell?"

Quaint touched one of the panels, a fingertip tracing the mother-of-pearl of the intarsia. She hated that cabinet in particular, and had tried to remove it from the office several times, but it was so heavy, antiquated, and dark that it looked like a shadow encrusted to the wall.

"When we met, Erik was a boy of twenty-three, clever beyond his age, and he discovered on his own what I was, which amused me. At the time, I believed him to be kind, curious, and intelligent, and I thought there would be no issue in introducing him to my world. Let's say he aged like a rotten apple."

"Rotten," repeated Ariadne. "That's not how I remember him."

Instead, her memories were of books with annotations made on the sides of every page, entire dialogues they had written around literary or academic texts, questioning or agreeing with the content or one another. Erik had talked to her like an equal; he had believed there was something she could be, something more than a helpless, decaying cocoon of a person . . .

"That's not how I wanted to remember him either." Quaint removed his jacket, leaving it folded over the chair. "Erik has his qualities, I guess, but it would be a lie if I didn't say I disagree with most of his scientific curiosities, or whatever he calls them nowadays."

The thread. Ariadne could still hear Erik's placid and constant voice, the only stimulus in what felt like an endless night. *You need to follow the thread.*

Quaint cracked his shoulders and neck.

"What about you? Erik rarely interacts with other humans."

"When I was younger, I had a health complication and he helped me recover." Ariadne was surprised by the coldness of her voice. Erik said she had been unconscious for almost a week when he brought her to the house, and he was almost quitting when she finally woke up. "I owe him everything I have. My home, my job, my body, my knowledge . . . Even the protection of the guls of this street. I wouldn't be alive if it weren't for him."

"I see."

Quaint placed both hands on the side of the cabinet, lifting it as easily as he would have lifted the furniture of a dollhouse. Behind it, on the dusty wall spotted with mold, was a door she had never seen before.

"Ariadne." Quaint dusted his clothes and inserted the key into the hole. "I don't know what he keeps here. There might be things . . ."

"Yes?"

"Never mind."

Ariadne watched as he unlocked the door.

The storage room was as big as a comfortable bathroom and was crammed with countless objects: piled suitcases, a trunk, a small chest of drawers, a rack with several articles of clothing, and prototypes of arms and legs, thrown around like amputated limbs. Quaint turned on the light, and the cat observed them from the office.

Ariadne stopped in front of a tattered satchel with a red cross. Next to the satchel was a military uniform, old and green, and a pilotka with a red star. Ariadne held the jacket in the air, the sleeves longer than her arms, and stared at the single medal on its chest.

"Red Army," said Quaint, as if that was the most natural response in the world. "From 1945, I believe."

He took a bunch of papers from the trunk, and several black-and-white pictures fell to the floor. Ariadne knelt to look at the people in one of them. A young man with blond hair and horn-rimmed glasses smiled on a bench, and a middle-aged white woman laughed by his side, the finger wave of her short bob appearing under her hat. Someone had written over the picture with beautiful calligraphy:

To my darling Erik
With love, Genebra
Buenos Aires, Summer of 1953

"Genebra and I lived in Paris during the war," said Quaint, stretching his neck to look at the picture. "I don't remember much of this time. I guess my worst memories of Erik have overwritten the best ones."

"That's impossible." The man in the photo had the same smile as Erik, the same long nose, the same thin lips, the same down-turned eyes. "Erik can't be older than fifty."

"Born in 1923, actually."

She wanted to laugh, but she was only able to grimace. "He would be more than a hundred . . ."

Quaint stared intensely at her. Ariadne wondered what he saw behind the round black lenses—did he see a frail rabbit, hideous and frightened? An unpleasant human woman who couldn't smile? The promise of food? A naive and inexperienced child?

He started to collect the pictures scattered on the floor, piling one on top of the other.

"Erik isn't a gul, if that's what you're wondering."

"Then how . . . ?"

"Maybe we should leave that story for another day." Quaint offered a cryptic smile, mouth pressed in a taut line. Ariadne moved to another photo. A man leaned on the railing of a balcony, a cigarette resting comfortably between his tattooed knuckles. Smoke escaped from his lips, blurring the image of the city behind him.

"You haven't changed at all."

"How kind of you."

"Quaint."

"I should have warned you," he said. "I assumed you knew that Erik is older than he looks."

"No, he never . . ."

"I'm very sorry. It was insensitive of me not to ask."

Suddenly, the storage room felt too small for the two of them, and Ariadne crawled over to the chest of drawers, dirt clinging to her sweatpants.

"Anything there?"

"Notebooks," said Ariadne, waving one with a leather cover. "Many notebooks."

"Ah!" That caught Quaint's attention, and he stooped behind her to look at the contents of the drawer over her shoulder. "His journals. Those might help."

In her memories, Erik was constantly drawing or writing, but she never knew to what extent. Countless pages written in Russian, realistic sketches made in pencil with diminutive notes next to them, folded newspaper articles, crumpled toffee wrappers, and dried plants that turned to dust when she touched them. She even found a drawing of Quaint: the sunglasses, the tattoos, the smile. Erik had taught her how to read Cyrillic script, but thousands of cursive handwritten lines were a little bit of a challenge for her, and she had to focus to understand.

"Were you born during the Ming dynasty?"

Quaint, who had already moved to another box, turned around immediately, and Ariadne allowed herself a rare smile. There were two things most guls considered too private to share: their age, and eating full meals in front of others.

"It's you." She pointed at the scribbled lines. "'*Quaint, a Chinese gul born sometime during the Ming dynasty. A well-traveled diplomat.*' There's something else, but I can't understand it."

"Yes, that's me."

"I suppose Quaint is not your real name."

Quaint chuckled, taking the diary from her hands to read what Erik had written there.

"It's not. Some of us guls have this impertinent habit of changing names from time to time. My wife used to call me Quaint, and it stuck." He played with one of the rings on his left hand. "Maybe someday I'll tell you my other names."

"Are you married?" Ariadne raised an eyebrow. She couldn't imagine what kind of woman a man like him would like.

"Widowed. But I was married, yes, more than once, in one way or another." Quaint pulled every journal out of the drawer, checking the dates on the spines. "Here, from last year! '*Tomorrow, I will go to Genebra's house, but I must leave the journals behind. I can't stop thinking of their proposal. What do I need to do to be left alone? I don't want to do this again. I caused enough harm . . .*'"

"Wait—Erik left years ago."

"That's not what he wrote. There's more: '*I'm not brave enough to talk to Ariadne, but I won't run away anymore. I'm often drowning in guilt whenever I come to the clinic without telling her, but I know it's the right choice: they don't know about it, and Boniface and Terebê swore they would keep her safe. The last thing I would want is to see her involved in this nonsense.*'"

Ariadne took the journal from his hands. How dare he?

How dare he enter the house while she slept without telling her? He knew she rarely ever left. How could she rest now, knowing someone had gotten into the apartment and she had not even noticed? She turned the page and found something else written in pencil:

Quaint, if you're here, I need your help again.
There are people who know what I did in 1972, but I won't say a word. Promise.
I will ask for help in Cabaré.
E.

Ariadne glanced at Quaint from the corner of her eye. The man repeated the words again and again without a sound.

"What does that mean?"

"It means that someone took Erik," answered Quaint. "And, if what he wrote is true, the situation is worse than I could have imagined."

You need to follow the thread, somebody whispered in her ear, caressing the thick dark hair on her forehead. Ariadne woke up, or thought she did; her mind was awake, but her body was tied to the mattress by invisible chains. *You need to follow the thread, Ariadne*, the voice continued, and heavy claws choked the air out of her.

Ariadne moved a finger. At first, she feared breaking it, but her consciousness reminded her that all her limbs could be fixed, starting from her lower thighs to the tips of her toes, and from above her elbows to her hands. She continued the movements until she was able to open and close her fist, and she kicked the duvet away, exhausted.

Ribbons of light invaded the bedroom through the venetian blinds, and the tablet on the nightstand announced the time: eleven in the morning. How long since she stopped having that dream? Ariadne sat on the bed, massaging her thighs and observing the intersection of flesh and carbon fiber. Erik's invention bordered on perfection: robotic arms and legs that allowed full mobility, removable synthetic skin, a neural implant, and delicate waterproof sensors that allowed her to experience heat, pressure, and even pain.

All of that made just for her. First, for her teenage body, then for the adult woman she became. *I just want your life to be as comfortable as possible*, Erik had said, petting her hair. He also taught her how to maintain and update them, so she wouldn't depend only on him. *If I can help you a tiny little bit, I'll be the happiest man on earth.*

Ariadne touched her own skin like Erik used to, her head raspy against her palm. Even her bangs, black and sweaty, had been part of the dream . . . By her side, the tablet blinked with a notification under Quaint's name, reminding her of his ominous words:

> I've been trying to contact Genebra, but a friend in common told me he has not seen her in a year.
> Can I bring you lunch?

Her answer was a dull "yes" before she entered the shower. Scalding water eased the pain but didn't erase the thought that haunted her like the voice of her dreams: *You're allowing a gul inside your house.* Ariadne slipped on her pants and walked to the office with a towel around her shoulders. So what if she did? What was the worst thing that could happen?

Look at you, Erik again, his voice pitiful and sweet. *Look at you.* Now it was her, checking the robotic articulations exposed without the skin. *It has nothing to do with guls,* Ariadne answered herself, furious for even humoring the doubt. She was nothing like the amputated advisers on TV. Her limbs, her life, had nothing to do with them. *Stop making things up.*

If she tried, she could see Erik opening the door, but the office was exactly like they had left it the previous day: the cabinet had been pushed aside, the storage area was unlocked, and the papers were disorganized over the desk. It wasn't the Erik of the photos, but the one of her memories: light hair sprinkled with gray falling over his eyes while he worked, sun-spotted skin, a straight nose that pointed down, a narrow mouth that smiled too well.

But Erik wasn't there. He had been, while she slept, or on the rare occasions she left the building. He had spoken to Terebê downstairs, broken into the apartment, pushed aside a gigantic cabinet, left his belongings inside the storage room. And then disappeared again. Ariadne sighed. Quaint sent another message saying he would be there soon, so she went back to the bedroom to put on her skin, bra, and shirt before going downstairs.

The intercom rang ten minutes later, and he crossed the threshold with paper bags smelling like moqueca capixaba.

"I hope I made the right choice" was the first thing Quaint said, leaving the bags on the living room table. "Since I can't actually eat it, I tend to choose based on what smells good and looks nice."

Quaint had brought more food than any person could possibly need: a bowl full of salad, another with white rice, a third of pirão paste, some plantain, and a container of fish stew garnished with chives, parsley, and onion, along with a box of Belgian truffles.

"Do I look like I eat this much?" Ariadne set the table for two, even if he was just going to watch. Quaint adjusted his dark glasses with a finger, the corners of his lips turning up.

"I might have been accused of overdoing it in the past."

"Did *you* eat?" The question sounded casual enough, and Quaint's smile grew.

"Two weeks ago. Worried about my diet?"

"I want to know if I smell like food to you." She helped herself to a generous portion of moqueca. An adult male who ate fourteen days ago could either spend the whole month without eating, or eat again in less than a week. "How many fangs do you have?"

Quaint laughed and threw his head back, his Adam's apple going up and down. From that distance, she could see how massive his canines were.

"Ten pairs, Doctor. Is it worrying?"

"To me it is. To you, it's excellent. The guls I've treated so far had four pairs at most. Erik said the average is six." Stewed fish and tomato melted on her tongue, and she nodded, pleased. "The damage must be impressive."

"My mother had an astonishing eleven at her peak, and my father had seven. You should see the wreckage that tiny little creature could cause in her day." Quaint scratched his chin, rings glowing under the light. "Even I was scared of her when I was a child. Not that she's any less threatening with eight pairs."

"*Is?*" Ariadne narrowed her eyes, trying to imagine his mother to no avail. "Present?"

"Present, yes." Quaint swallowed another chuckle. "Sometimes, I think she'll outlive me. Last year, she made it a promise . . ."

"I'm sure she's fascinating."

"But rest assured, Ariadne, I don't feel any joy in terrorizing harmless humans, nor in mistreating them. I only eat those I deem deserving of it."

"Meaning I shouldn't get on your bad side."

"You can disrespect me and loathe me as much as you want." Quaint pressed his lips together. "Still, the bar is set above petty disagreements. I only eat the violent and truly dreadful. If I never considered Erik for a meal, I doubt you'd end up on my list. You're far more pleasant company than he is."

"Is this about what happened in 1972?"

Quaint joined his hands, reflecting for a few seconds before answering.

"No—it's about our last clue. Have you ever heard of Cabaré?"

"Once, but I don't know much about it," said Ariadne. Erik had told her about it when she was a teenager, and described it as the most traditional gul club in Brazil, built three centuries ago and remodeled a few times since. *It's an interesting little place, frequented by the gul elite and powerful people,* Erik had explained with a thoughtful smile, *but I wouldn't recommend humans go there.* "Do you think they did something against him?"

"I doubt it, but the others might know something," answered Quaint. "I'll be in Rio in two days to find out."

Her lips parted, trying to form a response. Quaint had appeared in her life without a warning, different from anyone she had ever met, different from Erik, from herself. Part of her wanted to laugh with relief, glad to be back to her little routine, where she hid inside the house and pretended the years were not passing and the clock was not ticking, stuck in an endless cycle of repetitive days. She would not know what had happened to Erik; she would only be given a report later, from the mouth of someone else.

Ariadne closed the plastic boxes to put them in the fridge. "What about your tattoos?"

"The tattoos can wait."

Quaint looked like he intended to say something else, but gave up before he even tried. He got up to help her with the dirty dishes.

"I'll let you know if I have any news."

The day dragged after Quaint left. In less than forty-eight hours, her life would continue to be the same as it always was. Wherever Erik had vanished to, if he was in danger, Quaint would solve everything by himself. Ariadne extracted one of Boniface's damaged molars, left food outside for the stray cats, and, at night, she turned on the television to watch the news after curfew. The whistle blew religiously at nine in every neighborhood, and she preferred to distract herself to avoid thinking of what happened in the streets at night. She believed, in part, that the government had made a secret deal with the guls: after a certain hour, the world was there for the taking, far from curious eyes. But that didn't explain the mutilated advisers, or the squads that patrolled the streets for anyone they deemed unfit, from the homeless and the ill to those who broke the arbitrary laws that changed every other day.

"*. . . The Civil House released a memo stating that the president vehemently rejects any association of his person with death squads, and is solely focused on his recovery . . .*" Ariadne glanced at the TV as footage of the president entering the hospital from a helicopter from the previous month, looking horribly, humanly frail, appeared on-screen. *Serves him right,* she thought, unlocking the tablet and typing an answer to Quaint's last message, then deleting it. "*. . . The* *president continues to be under observation after a hip fracture. Tomorrow, the vice president . . .*"

Ariadne typed again, but this time she pressed send:

> Quaint, are you going tomorrow? I need to ask you something.

Three dots appeared under his name, but instead of a message, she received a new call. Ariadne accepted it without thinking, and his face appeared on the screen. Quaint, still wearing his round sunglasses, a strand of black hair falling over his forehead, and tattoos up his long neck, with the elegant yet nondescript wall of his hotel room looming in the background. He was watching the same news on his TV: "*The armed forces have arrived in São Paulo today to control an insurgence of protests . . .*"

Quaint smiled when he saw her.

"Good evening," he said. "I see we are doing the same thing."

Ariadne muted the TV. "This channel is horrible, turn it off."

"But we're not going to talk about the news, are we?" joked Quaint, the image blurring as he moved to turn off the television.

"Erik helped me when I needed it." Ariadne tried to ignore her ugly little face in the corner of the video call. She held the tablet in the air, feeling like her wrists were about to glitch under the weight of it, and she convinced herself that the pain was not real, just an illusion of the implant. "I want to help him, too."

Quaint didn't answer. With the glasses, it was hard to guess what he was thinking, but she took his solemn expression as encouragement to continue:

"Take me with you, please."

On the television, the news had been replaced by ads: a family enjoyed a particular brand of coffee, then it changed to an obligatory health campaign. Finally, Quaint answered with a reassuring smile:

"Two heads are better than one."

II

Curfew

Something moved inside her body. First slowly, almost softly, brushing against her entrails and compressing her organs. Her initial discomfort turned into pain, pulling and twisting, and she covered her mouth, afraid to throw up. A muffled noise startled her—a bubble bursting, a pop, the sound of dripping water.

Out, Ariadne thought, *out.*

Only then did she notice volume in her abdomen that should not have been there. Her belly was large and round, her breasts swollen and heavy, her knees seared with pain. *No,* she thought, horrified, scratching the stretched skin to remove whatever had invaded her gut. *Out, out, out,* she screamed, or she thought she did, droplets of blood sprouting from her belly button.

It can't be happening. Ariadne slapped herself one, two, three times on her stomach and face. *Not to me.* The words blurred into tears while she pulled, pinched, cut. It was unbearable, the feeling of being touched at all times, of having no control over what came and went inside her. She wanted to be small, invisible, intangible, she wanted . . .

"Ariadne?"

Ariadne opened her eyes. Her entire body was sore, and she found it hard to breathe. Quaint waited for her outside of the taxi, holding the door open.

"I fell asleep," she mumbled, accepting his hand to exit the car. He had his own suitcase in his other hand, a second bag with the journals they had taken from the storage room, and her duffel bag hung from his other arm. "I'm sorry."

"Don't apologize," said Quaint, walking with long strides. He had picked her up at the clinic after Ariadne left the cat with Terebê, and they went together to Vitória Airport, passing by several police cars blasting their sirens. "The trip is short, but you can sleep during it as well."

"Where are we going to stay in Rio?"

"I took the liberty of booking a hotel in Copacabana."

"Must have cost an arm and a leg."

It was challenging to follow Quaint, short as she was, but she tried her best to keep up with him. Whenever they stopped at a queue, she glanced at travelers pushing their carts, mothers taking children by the hand, soldiers—human, apparently, flat-toothed and oblivious—with rifles standing in front of every gate.

"Money is not an issue," replied Quaint. "Let me worry about that, yes?"

It was impressive how he moved with ease even in hostile environments, dodging bodies and taking the passport and the tickets from his jacket, both attentive and agile. Ariadne didn't even know if she had ever traveled by plane before. She guessed she had, based on the questions asked by Erik when she woke up in his house, hurt and disoriented. *What's your name? Where are your parents? Any information can help: address, city, phone . . .*

Ariadne walked through the metal detector after discreetly showing them her prosthesis card. *I don't have a name*, she had lied. *I don't have a family. I don't know where I was born.* She had lied so many times that the real memories dissolved, and her lie became true. *That's not my name*, she repeated to herself every time the old one returned to her head. *I'm no longer her.*

"Ariadne?" Quaint's voice distracted her from her thoughts. She looked up to meet his eyes, and her neck twitched in pain. "Are you nervous?"

"I'm fine." She crumpled her identity card. The Ariadne in the picture was the same Ariadne who had fooled Erik so well: young, exhausted, with dark hair and unfocused eyes. "I've never been to the airport before."

"I see." Quaint began to walk more slowly, and offered his arm. "Hold me."

"Quaint?"

"Indulge me, please."

Ariadne held the sleeve of his mustard shirt, and Quaint covered her hand with his, gently forcing her to hold his arm. Around them, the human traffic only increased as they walked from one gate to another, and she noticed there were more armed soldiers on the airfield runway. She hid her face against him, drowned by the scent of his cologne, by the softness of the fabric and the warmth that, no matter how inhuman, was alive, alive like she was . . . Ariadne only noticed they had reached the plane when she heard the flight attendants greeting them at the door—*Good afternoon, sir, good afternoon, ma'am, good afternoon, good afternoon*—and Quaint brushed her fingers slightly.

"Would you like the window seat?" he asked, standing in front of the two seats of the first row. "So you can enjoy the view when we get to Rio."

Ariadne sat down. Quaint placed his suitcase in the overhead bin, and she closed her eyes one more time, consumed by the horrible sensation that insects were crawling from her shoulders to her neck, from her thighs to the middle of her legs, countless fingers skimming across her.

Fingers that grabbed, groped, seized; punched, hit, slapped; fingers that curled around her throat and choked. Fingers that were part of a hand, a large and sturdy hand that kept her immobile under a heavy body that breathed over her, panting the name that she stubbornly believed no longer belonged to her. He had said it so many times that she had started to dread that hideous word, and begged others to call her by any other name . . .

"You can hold on to me again," whispered Quaint. Ariadne touched his shirt, staring at the sleeves he had just rolled up. Her eyes stopped at one of his tattoos. A woman's hairpin, carefully adorned with delicate flowers, resting forever on the skin of his inner arm.

She traced the tattoo, and Quaint smiled.

"What is it?"

"The hairpin of my first love." Quaint looked at the dark screen in front of him. "She broke it in half and left one of the parts with me, but I never had the chance to give it back."

"One of your wives?"

"In our hearts, yes. Unfortunately, it's not what life had

in store." Quaint tapped one of the flowers with a finger. "I don't know how many times I've redone this tattoo since."

Ariadne imagined what the pin must have looked like in real life: thin, jade inlay, and gold wire, with a ruby as the centerpiece, carefully arranged in someone's long hair.

"Every time you get one, your immune system breaks it down and removes the metal of the ink." Ariadne flipped his hand to see the other images. "I'd say the only reason you're able to keep them for even a few years is because your regeneration process accelerates when you're in danger, and a tattoo is just a minor wound. Essentially, you're torturing yourself."

"Everyone deals with their memories the way they can."

Quaint offered a reassuring smile, as if saying those exhausting pain sessions were something he could take, and Ariadne spent the following thirty minutes in a state of near sleep. Her mind wandered, imagining what it would be like to live for centuries like they did. Guls believed that everyone, human and nonhuman, was part of a reincarnation cycle that involved different places, bodies, and times. Erik believed it, too, and said he had made the same friends in many lives: in the Soviet Union, England, Morocco, Italy, China. *Their presence made me more sensitive, spiritually speaking*, Erik had claimed. *I often have dreams of the past, sometimes with lives that are not even mine . . . Maybe some of them are yours, don't you think?*

"We're almost there."

Galeão Airport was already crammed with people when they arrived, but most were part of a tactical unit lined up for a flight to São Paulo. Quaint headed straight to the queue of yellow taxis outside, ignoring the large number of police officers, and sat in the passenger seat after helping the driver with the luggage.

The radio was on, but she absorbed only a few fragments of the news:

". . . trails of blood in the avenue, and the police are now investigating . . . Nongovernmental organizations have alleged that the number of missing sex workers and homeless people in large cities has increased again, but the president argues that this is a ploy invented by the opposition to . . ."

"Can you please turn off the radio?" Quaint pulled down the sun visor as news of the amputation of the arm of a minister after a supposed accident began. Ariadne had the impression that he was looking at her through the reflection. Quaint seemed to tense up every time he heard the news, reminding her of the anger bristling in Boniface after the visit of a death squad. The driver lowered the volume to a minimum. "Thank you."

Ariadne relaxed, grateful. Just to be sure, she checked the inside of her purse. Besides her documents, money, and medication, she had brought a case with carfentanil vials and several syringes. *It's, um, an old party trick*, Erik had said when he taught her how to falsify the labels and store the tranquilizer in the most discreet way possible. *We might be weaker than them, but even a gul will go down for a few days with this.*

She thought again of all those humans who, by all means, seemed like they were being eaten alive, but by whom, really? Why would a gul choose such public victims? *Don't think of it*, she thought, glancing at Quaint. *Not here.*

Outside, the sky was growing darker, and the evening blue was spotted with a few gray clouds. The palm trees cast shadows on the pavement, and the taxi stopped in front of a sizable hotel facing the beach. It was a sumptuous building, and the white facade must have been lovely during the day, but at 7:40 p.m. the lights in the windows were almost all on, and all she could see was the large frame of the sober construction.

"Come," called Ariadne. "We need to go before curfew."

"Guls don't have curfew," Quaint answered with a strange smile. He carried their luggage by himself, and had looked thoroughly offended when she said she could carry hers. "Speaking of which . . ."

"The news?"

"How did you know?"

"You're easy to read." Ariadne followed him to the entrance, where two porters rushed to help.

"Is that so! Maybe I am easy to read indeed." Quaint thanked the porter and murmured something in his ear. "Or perhaps I have lost my touch. But we'll speak more at dinner, yes?"

They crossed the antique revolving door, and Ariadne felt immediately uncomfortable. The floor was polished marble and glittered under the chandelier, a carpet went from the entrance to the top of the stairway, and the front desk clerks whispered to each other, observing them. Unlike her, Quaint looked like he had been made for this scenario, or that the scenario had been crafted for him: his brogues against the caramel lozenges of the flooring, the light reflected in his black hair, his tailored suit as carefully planned as the uniform of the clerks.

I know some people here, he explained when they were alone in the Edwardian elevator. Guls, she knew, by the way he avoided looking at her.

The suite was almost a house of its own: it had two bedrooms, each with their own bathroom, and a living room that included a desk, a sofa, and a table or two, along with a balcony facing the Atlantic Ocean. Ariadne thought she would have to dine there, but Quaint insisted they try one of the three restaurants inside the hotel instead.

"I thought of taking you to the Italian one," he said with amusement, taking only his wallet. "But the clerk told me that one is usually fuller, and I wanted privacy."

The restaurant he had in mind was almost empty, maybe because other guests were trying to enjoy the little time they had before curfew, maybe because the new law discouraged those who wanted to go out at night. The maître d'hôtel led them to a more secluded table behind a pair of translucent curtains, and Quaint offered her the cushioned seat.

A waiter handed him the menu as soon as they sat, like Ariadne didn't even exist.

"Oh, no, please give it to the lady, I already ate." Quaint pulled the string that tied the curtains, hiding their table from view, and unbuttoned the collar of his shirt. "So. About the news."

"Go on."

"I'm sure you agree that this curfew nonsense is too convenient for guls," said Quaint. The guardian lion on his neck had already lost the vivid blackness of the first day, like a tattoo done in recent years. "It keeps our best interests in mind: no one knows we're involved, and we keep . . . well, we keep eating."

"I think about it all the time." Ariadne looked at the candles on the table, discreetly moving her hand away from them. "That and the mutilations."

"Yes, that's another pressing issue. It feels too . . . crass for guls." Quaint paused, thoughtful. "I'll investigate those so-called death squads tonight. They might have something to do with Erik's work."

"They're not guls," Ariadne hurried to say, remembering Boniface's cafe. "They're human."

"Yes, but they probably have an agreement with guls on the side. It's not unheard of." Quaint glanced at the approaching waiter, and stretched his neck to read the items on the menu. "Don't you want to try the tasting menu? I'm dying to see all the dishes."

"You better not die on me tonight," Ariadne whispered irritably. "I can't afford to get back home."

Quaint laughed like a child. "I'm not afraid of humans."

"Maybe you should be," she retorted, then stopped talking when the waiter came to write down her order. "If you're so keen on wasting money, I'll have the tasting menu with dessert."

"You heard her," said Quaint, the same mischievous smile playing on his lips.

"What about other guls?" Ariadne asked when the waiter had left. "Are you afraid of them?"

His grin grew with the question. Ariadne felt like ripping the sunglasses off his face, as if they were the key to understanding his intentions. Quaint scratched his chin, looking at the lightbulbs in the ceiling, and she stared at him, waiting.

"It would be unwise not to be, but I'm not only excessive, I'm also quite insolent . . ."

"I noticed."

"You're not supposed to agree!" Another audacious laugh, but there was no arrogance in it. "I have friends at Cabaré, Ariadne, and I know how to keep the ones that are not my friends far from me."

Ariadne smiled back. "Maybe you're the one who has a temper."

"Touché."

The sound of running water distracted her from the quietness of the outside world. Ariadne burst one of the bubbles, inhaling the strong herbal scent coming from the foam as more warm water filled the porcelain interior of the tub, clear except for the bath infusion she had gotten from the reception desk. Quaint had left one hour ago, when they heard the high-pitched whistle of the police car patrolling the neighborhood that announced curfew was about to start.

Don't do anything reckless, Ariadne had told him in the corridor before he disappeared down the emergency stairs. Quaint had simply waved his hand, back turned to her: *You won't even notice my absence.*

After that, the hotel locked the front doors, the elevator stopped bringing guests to the ground floor, and most of the windows were closed tight. Nothing could be heard from outside, like Rio de Janeiro was a ghost town, except for the crashing waves and occasional scream.

Ariadne sat on the edge of the tub and started to peel off her skin.

First, she removed the layer that went from her lower left thigh to her foot, then she unrolled the soft synthetic skin of her right leg. She did the same with her two arms, pulling the fingertips slowly from the fake nails, and washed them with water and soap before putting everything back in place. The sensors in her prosthetic limbs were as connected to her brain as her biological nerves, allowing her to move and feel at will, and they were the result of the aggressive rehabilitation Erik had planned for her.

A new thought disturbed her: he couldn't have done all of that alone. It was too dangerous. If she was right, and he hadn't, who had helped Erik take her out of there?

Ariadne remembered a human couple who had been part of her recovery. The husband, João, was a well-known gynecologist from Fortaleza, and the wife, Irene, was a psychiatrist specializing in post-traumatic stress disorder. They were both attentive and kind, but the idea that a gul might have been involved in secret made her stomach churn. *He wouldn't have betrayed my trust like that*, she thought, but inside she knew it wasn't true. Erik had invaded the apartment without telling her, just to leave his journals in the storage space.

Before she realized it, she was back in the living room, searching for Erik's journals. Quaint had left some on the desk, and she skimmed through the labels to find the ones from the late 2000s. Ariadne took them back to the bathroom and got into the tub, leaning against the tiles and holding one of the journals with her dry hand.

The girl's progress is excellent, at least concerning her physical health. She's taking the appropriate medicine for phantom pain, and seems to have fun in our physiotherapy sessions! She also accepts food now, even if a little unwillingly.

João delivered me her results yesterday. Negative for STDs, but I already imagined that. Genital and anal trauma, hematomas, etc., are almost all healed (what a relief!), but the yeast infection has both of us worried. She might find the treatment too invasive . . .

Ariadne closed the notebook. That was not what she wanted to read.

The girl woke up!!! read an older entry. She remembered vaguely the feeling of waking up in a house she had never seen before, her body unspeakably sore and what remained of her limbs refusing to move. *Good morning*, Erik had said with a low and soothing voice. *No, no, please, don't be afraid! No one will hurt you again.*

At the time, her mind had been vacant. So empty, in fact, so shielded from any possible harm, that she could barely recall the year, and had to make a conscious effort to place Erik's notes in her own timeline.

She refuses to say her name. Irene also tried to convince her to talk so we could at least find her parents, Erik had written. *She claims she can't remember, but I feel she might be lying . . .*

Ariadne turned the page, touching the blue ink and leaving a damp fingerprint on the paper.

Amazing! Despite G. (for Girl! He-he) having forgotten so many things, she remembers what I said when she was still unconscious.

Follow the thread, Ariadne . . . Who would have thought that, of all the things I have ever done, a harmless reference would have been the one thing stored by her brain? I find it comforting that she doesn't need to think of the horrible things that have been done to her.

The journal of the first year was mostly tidbits of her recovery and ideas for prosthetic limbs. *Despite the leg amputation not being very recent (I'd say it must have been done a few years before now, but I can't know for sure), G. is already used to her new movements*, wrote Erik, *but I want more for her. I want her to have her freedom back.* It also had drawings, like the one she saw of Quaint.

One depicted Ariadne, reading a book on the sofa, her hair in a short bob, her face small and round, the stumps of her thighs visible without the robotic legs. He wrote *Ariadne, 15* under the sketch, and a small annotation on the corner of the page: *(A quadruple amputation; the arms are prototypes. She found them "weird." I'll fix that later.)*

On another page, months later, she found another interesting entry:

Sometimes, I have nightmares about the children I was not able to save. When that happens, I find myself returning to the old habit of praying before bed, a habit I thought was as lost as the parts of me I left in Stalingrad . . .

Guls believe we reincarnate in groups of similarly minded people, and that we meet our loved ones in life after life. I hope they are right, and that the ones who died can come back as tabulae rasae, one day, one day . . .

Ariadne yawned, drying herself with a towel and dressing while she read. She had vague memories of other children who cried too much, brought by a man in a hat, and the impression that they never stayed for long. Sometimes, she convinced herself she had been born in the house where she was found, and while she knew she hadn't been, it was true that she had grown from childhood into adolescence in the nightmare that still visited her from time to time.

She lay on the sofa to read, but words and sketches merged inside her head, becoming chimeras of facts. A massive, brutish man taking her to the garden of his house when she still could walk. Erik wrapping a duvet around her shoulders on a cold night. Finding medicine books in the office upstairs and reading them for weeks until Erik finally agreed to teach her. Ladyfingers if she was good, and *you're so, so good* whispered in her ear with a wet kiss, the sound of it muffled by the opening song of an afternoon telenovela. A man taking off his top hat when he entered the house.

You won't believe who I found hiding my books under her pillow, Erik had told Irene when he thought she was sleeping. *Smart little thing, isn't she?*

A girl with no limbs and no face, but it wasn't her. *No*, she thought, and the image was gone. Gone, gone, and the world became Erik again. *Keep following the thread, Ariadne*, written affectionately in a book about the myth of Theseus given on her sixteenth birthday, when she decided that she would keep that name. The 2014 World Cup, and how she had wept when Brazil conceded the fourth of seven goals to Germany. *No, no, no*, Erik turning off the television despite having joked that he would cheer for the European team before the match had started, shocked to finally see her cry. *Come here, let me hug you.*

How she had craved Erik's attention, and despised him for giving her a life she never asked to have. A life where she was not wanted—*he wanted me before*—where she was not touched—*why can't you touch me? I only exist if you touch me*—where she was only a child—*why now, why not then?* A life where Erik was the only man worth loving, and the only one who wouldn't do anything to her. It shouldn't have been like this—*I was only good enough to get fucked, now I'm nothing, why did you take this from me?*—she should have been dead, dead with the other kids, dead with *him*.

But I didn't ask to live! I don't want *to be happy!* It was she who was shouting. She had shattered a glass against the wall and scratched the synthetic skin of her arms to no avail. She could feel him on her, his touch, his voice, his orders, crawling on her body like the legs of a spider. He was even in the new limbs. And Erik's eyes, his sad blue eyes, looking at her while he swept up the shards.

The answer came from her: *I didn't mean . . . I'm sorry, Erik . . .*

Ariadne woke up to the sound of footsteps. The journal had been set aside, her cheeks were marked with the lines of a pillow, and the sky was still dark outside. For a second, she thought the prostheses were malfunctioning, but soon she realized she was just tired and in pain.

"Quaint?" Her body was heavy and sluggish, and Ariadne barely managed to sit down. "I'm sorry, I started to read and dozed off—"

She stopped speaking.

The man standing in the entrance of the room was the same man she had met at the clinic, but something wasn't right. His hair, usually slicked back, was disheveled, and his jacket and shirt were gone. From his usual clothes, only the white undershirt and the pants remained, but both were stained with blood.

"I didn't want you to see me like this." Quaint ran his dirty fingers through his hair. She realized the rings were gone as well, and he only wore the one with a golden crystal box and a lock of dark brown hair. "I thought you'd be in your room."

Ariadne froze. She tried to tell herself that he was still Quaint, that nothing had changed, but the dried blood gluing wild strands to his forehead made her body vibrate in alarm.

The gul left his shoes at the entrance of the suite, and she flinched instinctively.

"You're afraid of me."

"No." Ariadne spoke too fast. Part of her, a detached and curious part that didn't want to pretend she wasn't there, wanted to know what kind of person he had eaten, and if that would have any effect on his health. *Like Ms. Terebê and her diabetes*, she thought stupidly, feeling like she was still in the middle of a dream. "I'm not."

"Can I come closer?"

Ariadne nodded. Even his smell was different, perfume and sweat and something metallic that bordered on sweet. Her eyes fell to the unbuckled belt as he walked toward her, the tattoos going from his fingers to his shoulders, the dark stain in his abdomen, as if someone had tried to grab him in the middle of their struggle. It was strange to see him like that, so uncovered, but it was also a reminder that she could not underestimate his strength.

"So?"

"A squad stopped me, you see." Quaint's belt went down with a *clack*, whipping the floor beneath her feet. "Human, all of them, like you said. Not too kind to foreigners, but that changed very quickly, when they *noticed.* Told me I was free to roam at night. Could even bring me food, like we were in a damn restaurant. That's what they call the politically unwanted. *Food.* Sounds very planned to me."

Ariadne's breathing was uneven and sparse, coming out in inaudible staccato gasps. Food. Food. Food. Could Erik be involved with this? No, they had taken him. Could he be forced to . . . No, he would not comply, would he?

"Nobody saw you?"

"Only the guls from the laundry." Quaint raised her chin with his index finger, and the proximity made her realize he had blood under his nails as well. "I thought you weren't afraid of me."

"Only if you give me good reason to be." Ariadne held his wrist, fingers curling into claws around the peony on the back of his hand. For a moment, she wanted to rip the tattoo off his skin and show those creatures they were not the only ones who could do harm, but the thought vanished as quickly as it came. "If you do, I won't forgive you."

Quaint smiled.

"Let's make it a promise, then."

Half-Eaten

The yellow house was not particularly interesting, but she recognized it as soon as she saw it, in the silent and almost magical understanding of dreams. Ariadne touched the walls with a gloved hand, feeling the stucco. She didn't know to whom it belonged—*to me, it belongs to me*—but she knew the corridors like the lines of her own veins. She wandered in the garden, under the shade of a guava tree, she ate a ladyfinger in the kitchen, she went upstairs.

There was a man strapped to a dental chair in one of the rooms. A man much larger than her. His lower teeth appeared through his lips and he had a protruding jaw, but after she anesthetized him, the man's face changed to Quaint's.

It was a shame, to extract such impressive teeth, but she took out his fangs one by one: canines, premolars, molars. *I'm doing this for you*, she said, but neither voice nor words were hers. *Mostly, I'm doing this for myself.*

Ariadne woke up. The hotel was white, not yellow, and a light sea breeze blew through the window, brushing her face.

She pulled the wires off her limbs. They had been charging since the previous night, after she took one more glance at Quaint's shadow before he disappeared into his own room. Ariadne headed to the bathroom and washed her face repeatedly.

The more she tried to ignore the horrible images from her dreams, the more they returned, indistinguishable from the ones of the night before: Quaint's stained undershirt, his dirty hand lifting her face, the smell of death that surrounded him. *They called them food.*

Ariadne took a few clothes from her luggage. Cabaré was located in the wealthiest part of the neighborhood of Flamengo and had been frequented for centuries by the gul elite. *Aren't they all elite, in a way?* she thought bitterly, wearing black leggings under a turtleneck dress. She wrapped a cardigan around herself to make sure no one would see any piece of her skin outside her face and hands, then checked her purse: phone, wallet, tranquilizers, pain meds.

To her surprise, Quaint wasn't outside. Guls rarely slept except for a few naps here and there, and only fell into slow wave sleep during their hibernation period, but they had agreed to go to Cabaré. His room was empty, the journals were still piled on the desk, the curtains of the terrace fluttered with the wind. Ariadne opened one of the notebooks out of curiosity, leafing through the pages of a journal from 1948.

Quaint—the word never rolls easily off my tongue, but I will learn, I will learn—promised to help with my French, but he can't help but laugh whenever I try to communicate with Parisians.

Unlike me, everything seems to come to him without effort:

his accent is flawless, his manners impeccable, and there is a certain unworldly aspect to him. It is both charming and unnerving, and reminds me always of my very human imperfection, in a way no other goule makes me feel.

Genebra laughed when I told her; says I flatter him way too much (but later, she admitted: "Quaint has always been like this").

Ariadne closed the journal, wondering if she could find any clue in Erik's first steps into the gul world as to how to deal with them. *Besides, he didn't respect my privacy either*, she thought with disdain.

"Miss Yurkova?" A hotel worker knocked outside. "There's a delivery for you."

"We haven't ordered *any*—" Ariadne stopped speaking when she opened the door. Her eyes fell on the bouquet in the man's arms: red roses wrapped in brown paper and twine, so many of them that the bright green leaves were escaping from their enclosure and several petals fell on the carpeted floor.

The clerk handed her a little envelope from the middle of the bouquet. "Have a good day."

She unfolded the note and stared at the elegant calligraphy on it, knowing exactly who had sent it as soon as she read the first line:

> *Ariadne,*
> *Please forgive me for last night. I would not like that to be the image you have of me.*
> *Waiting for you downstairs,*
> *Q.*

Ariadne smiled against her better judgment and left the flowers on the table before heading to the ground floor.

Quaint was on a leather sofa with his legs crossed, and he lowered the newspaper covering his face when she touched his arm.

"Apology accepted."

Quaint smiled, folding the paper and leaving it on the chair. "Ready?"

"As ready as I can be. Anything I should know before we go?"

"Cabaré is a three-story house." Quaint typed the address into the taxi app on his phone. "Invited humans can walk around freely on the first floor. On the second, you should be either accompanied by me, or have permission to go. The third floor, however . . ."

"What about it?"

"It's supposed to be a gul-only space, but that's . . . not always the case. If need be, I can take you, of course, but strangers would assume that I plan to eat you before the night ends. Or that you're mad."

"Mad it is."

"Don't make that face." Quaint locked his phone, and it disappeared into the pocket of his suit. "There's nothing strange on the first floor, and that's all we're seeing today."

When the taxi arrived, they sat side by side on the backseat, where a small television broadcast the news: . . . *The president has not been seen in public since his treatment started two months ago, sparking rumors of a terminal illness . . .*

"I get the curfew. One party eats, the other terrorizes and controls." Ariadne stared at the new headline: *Civil House criticized again after another assistant had their limbs amputated after a road accident . . .* "But what about them? What can a dying human tyrant get from all of this? And he is human—you know, I know—he's a leech that keeps aging as he grows in power. What can he get from this?"

"He's not afraid to sacrifice his own, *clearly*," commented Quaint, his voice low enough to be muffled by the wind. "And guls always take more and more."

"Quaint. If anything happens . . ."

"I'll protect you. Ten pairs, remember?"

"Ten pairs," Ariadne repeated dully. A dozen teeth scattered on a metal table, bloody and lifeless, like the ivory of elk. "You keep deflecting every time I ask about what happened in 1972. Is Erik's disappearance related to it?"

Quaint made a thoughtful sound. He was back to his usual self, with a cobalt-blue suit, rings on most fingers, and perfectly combed hair.

"That's a story for yet another day. We're here."

The car stopped in front of a mansion hidden by palm trees, with wrought iron gates that did little to conceal the majestic, eclectic architecture of the upper floors. The walls were coral, the tallest windows concealed by closed curtains despite the hour, and security guards—presumably human—watched the place. There were traces of movement on the ground floor, like a couple speaking or a child running, but the closer the windows were to the roof, the more they looked like they were guarding a graveyard.

"There is a Brazilian idiom I quite enjoy," said Quaint, fingers drumming on the brass knob when they reached the front door. "I heard it started long ago, when a fire consumed a brothel frequented by wealthy men. While the women ran outside to control the flames, the men's wives ran into the streets and yelled: 'Burn, cabaret!' It doesn't matter if it's true or not; every time a situation escalates, there's someone who will say that again, almost as if trying to induce the fire."

"What are you trying to say?"

"I'm saying that most guls are like that, Ariadne." Quaint offered his right arm gallantly, and Ariadne accepted it. "Most of us fall into one of two types. The first does damage control; we know we are harmful by nature, but we try to keep human suffering to a minimum. The others revel in causing pain."

Quaint opened the door.

The inside of the club was as ostentatious as the outside, and Ariadne was sure that the mansion had changed very little since its inception. There was an imperial staircase in the middle, where a feeble old woman walked arm in arm with a gul elder, chatting and seemingly unbothered by the predatory look cast upon her as they went to the second floor. Quaint guided her to the great hall of the first floor, where lunch was served to a handful of select human guests, but she saw glimpses of sunrooms, studies, and even a billiard room. A band played "Trem das Onze" upstairs, but the song was muffled by doors, ceilings, and walls, and all she could hear was the phantom melody mixed with chatter and laughter from the other tables.

Quaint pulled out her chair for her, but before she could sit, a thundering voice called his name:

"Why, why, if it isn't Quaint!" A short man displayed a wide smile. His Afro-textured hair was cropped and black, his skin was a very dark shade of brown, and his full beard covered half of his round face. "You didn't tell me you'd come for the ball. It's been a while!"

The newcomer pulled Quaint in for a friendly half hug.

"No parties for me this time." Quaint gave a courteous bow of the head. "Ariadne, meet Augusto, a good friend of mine. He's the first type I told you about."

Augusto kissed the back of her hand.

"A pleasure," he answered, then turned to Quaint with a frown in the middle of his bushy brow. "What are you saying behind my back?"

"It was a compliment, and I was not even thinking about you in the slightest," chuckled Quaint. "Augusto came from Mozambique to eat slavers, but ended up staying."

"And you went to France to eat Nazis." Augusto straightened his shirt, flattening the orange, yellow, brown, and white pattern. "Birds of a feather."

Ariadne glanced at the great hall. There were no more than fifteen people around, and she could spot the humans easily by the dishes in front of them: four middle-aged men spoke to a male gul at a nearby table, two elderly ladies laughed with an equally ancient female, a couple shared a settee near the piano, another talked on the veranda, and someone smoked in front of the window, admiring the view.

"Can I order you food?" asked Quaint, and Ariadne turned to him, nodding.

"The menu is all vegetarian." Augusto fetched a chair, sitting in front of Ariadne. "Or the humans find it suspicious."

Ariadne watched the guls in silence. Like Quaint and Augusto, all of them were gracious and well-dressed, the opposite of her.

"Augusto," she said after Quaint left. "Have you met Erik Yurkov?"

"Erik?" Augusto's droopy brown eyes analyzed her reactions, as if he knew she was doing the same to him. Then, he looked at Quaint over his own shoulder, watching as the other man called one of the waiters to show his membership card. "It was about time Quaint asked about him."

"Quaint didn't ask," replied Ariadne. "*I* did."

Augusto smirked. "And where do *you* know Erik from?"

"I'm his student." Ariadne touched one of the cloth napkins that had been rolled up to look like a blooming flower, crumpling it with her hand. "And I find it odd that he disappeared after coming here. Erik is no stranger to guls."

"Another doctor? How interesting, how very interesting . . ." Augusto seemed to consider her for the first time. "I agree with you; it *is* odd. Do you know Genebra?"

"I do," lied Ariadne.

"Genebra has a soft spot for Erik. Can't say no to him. Can't say no to anyone, in fact," he said with a shrug. "She told me some time ago that he asked to stay in her house for a while. Then both disappear into thin air."

"Did I miss anything?" Quaint returned, followed closely by a waiter who came carrying a drink and an entree.

"Told her my entire life," joked Augusto.

"Well, I've been meaning to ask . . ."

"About Erik? She already did."

"And? Do you know anything?"

"Not personally, but we could visit Genebra's place later." Augusto smiled behind his beard. "It's five minutes from here."

During lunch, Quaint and Augusto told her about all the people in the room. They started with Lena and Friedrich, a couple of German guls that had moved to Rio Grande do Sul in the early twentieth century and had collaborated with the military regime. Friedrich was rather ordinary, but the presence of Lena on the settee upset Ariadne, like an aged lioness waiting for prey.

Then, Ubirajara, the one by the window, with a long cream-colored dress that made him look like a 1940s movie star. *He sings when the choro band is not around*, Quaint explained in a whisper. Ubirajara waved lazily at them, holding a sharp cigarette holder between his fingers. *He's harmless*, said Augusto. *Or so he says.*

On the veranda, a sullen man reading the newspaper reclined on the alfresco sofa, and the woman by his side hugged his arm, looking at him adoringly. *Anzol is a translator from the Andes and Rosa is an heiress from Seville*, said Augusto, adding that they had fled Spain as soon as Franco died. *He might be a vulture, but he has her under his thumb.* Ariadne frowned. A vulture? *Guls who don't hunt*, explained Quaint. *They usually eat corpses from morgues, or the scraps of stronger guls.*

There was also a child Quaint recalled only vaguely, a plump little boy with dark hair, running and playing in the garden. For a human, he looked like he was seven or eight, but he wore a pair of antiquated shorts with a dress shirt, his fingers were full of tourmaline rings, and his growing deciduous fangs appeared whenever he laughed.

"Have you ever seen one of our children?" Augusto asked. "They're getting scarcer by the day."

"Only newborns. I'm aware he is older than me."

"Age is relative." Quaint observed the boy with a smile as he climbed the window to enter the great hall. "Yes, we develop slowly, but life passes as swiftly for him as it passes for a human child."

"How much time do you feel has passed for you?" asked Ariadne.

"I *know* how much time has passed, but I don't *feel* as old as you might see me. When I was a boy and made my first human friend, I told him we would see each other again very soon," explained Quaint. "When we met again, I was already an adolescent, and he had a great-granddaughter my age."

"Isn't it bad? Living with us?" Ariadne tried the chocolate mousse after the waiter came a third time, toying with the spoon on her lower lip. "We die too fast."

Augusto watched them talk with a strange look on his face.

"You learn how to process time differently. After this friendship, I started to pay attention, to nurture the moments I have with the humans I'm fond of. When they die, I keep them with me." Quaint traced the lines of the hairpin tattoo under the fabric of his shirt. "Hibernating for a decade when I'm grieving also helps."

Ariadne wanted to ask more about the hibernation period, in which a gul could spend years in a lethargic state after a sizable meal, but a noise distracted her. Someone stood up at the table full of businessmen to call a waiter, but she couldn't see his face. Quaint tensed up, and he exchanged a knowing glance with the other gul.

"You should go upstairs," suggested Augusto. "Let them know you're back. Sometimes, you learn a thing or two by acting friendly."

"Not with him," growled Quaint in a low voice.

"Not with him," Augusto agreed. "I can take the little lady to Genebra's house while you're there."

"Yes," Ariadne agreed, clutching her purse under the table to feel the sedative. "You said he's the first type, didn't you?"

The harshness vanished from his face, and Quaint offered a warm smile. "First type for sure. I'll meet you soon."

Erik has done this many times before, she told herself when she stepped out of Cabaré with Augusto. They walked past the guards toward the residential street, old mansion after old mansion save for a few apartments here and there. *He talked to guls, walked with guls*—Ariadne glanced at Augusto, who whistled and kept his hands shoved inside his pockets—*trusted guls.*

"Do you have the keys?"

"No, but I know where she keeps them." Augusto observed her from the corner of his eye as she took off her cardigan, revealing a pair of bare arms under the sleeveless dress. If she could, she would still be hidden under the clothes, but the weather was too warm. The man pointed at the prosthesis. "Erik's work, I take it?"

"Erik's work."

"The only thing that gives it away is a subtle line in the skin, but I wouldn't have noticed if I hadn't seen it in the sunlight," Augusto continued, seemingly unaware of her discomfort. "Quite the perfect job. When I kissed your hand, it felt warm."

"Don't tell Quaint, please."

"Sore spot?"

Ariadne didn't answer. There was no real reason to avoid telling Quaint; she felt no shame about having prosthetic limbs, nor did she remember how her original ones had felt. But, somehow, his knowing or not made her feel insecure, as if telling the truth could ruin the enchantment.

"Don't worry, I won't tell him," said Augusto. "How did it happen?"

Her fingers sank into the synthetic skin. Ariadne held his eyes for longer than she had to, trying to think of something to say. *I don't know* was not the right answer, because she did, sometimes, but any explanation felt fake.

"It's rude to ask."

"Is it?" Augusto stopped in front of one of the buildings, greeting the doorman as if he lived there. "My apologies."

Miss Genebra hasn't come home in a while, said the doorman, holding the door of the elevator. *Oh, she's taking care of her parents*, answered Augusto with a smile. *She asked me to pick up a few things before she's back.* When they reached the fourth floor, Augusto bent over to take the key from under a heavy Peruvian cactus pot and unlocked the apartment.

Despite the owner having been away for only a year, Genebra's apartment seemed frozen in time for more than a century. Even the wooden structure of the ceiling was old, as were the draped curtains, the gilded mirrors on the walls, the oil paintings, the Persian rugs on the floor. Augusto grimaced at the state of the furniture, covered in thick gray dust, and at the moldy spots on the wallpaper.

"Saying she hasn't been here in a while is an understatement." Ariadne touched a vanity in what she assumed was Genebra's bedroom. Some of the makeup on it was modern, as was the television in the living room and the air conditioner, but the rest was all from past decades.

"Some guls are stuck in time." Augusto opened the windows, and the smell improved slightly. "As a friend, Genebra is delightful. Very fun. Very kind. *But*—stuck in time. Mentally, I don't think she ever left the twenties. Well, the *last* twenties. I have lived plenty of those, myself, and now we're living another. Have you met her many times? Genebra?"

"I haven't, actually," admitted Ariadne. "I lied to you."

Augusto stopped checking the books on the nightstand, surprised. "*Really.*"

"I have my tricks."

The man started to laugh, one hand on his round belly.

"Forgive me for laughing, Ariadne, but you two are so different!"

"Me and who?"

"You and Erik, of course! You and Quaint . . . you seem to have more in common." Augusto walked around the four-poster, looking at the disheveled silk sheets. "I always thought Erik was an odd fellow. I told Quaint, but what's the use of telling him anything? He's soft in the heart. Always was. Especially with his humans."

"Why odd?"

"If you're close to Erik, you know what I mean. That thing he did, smiling all the time. Never saying what he truly thought. Always a little nervous, a little coy, a little too caught red-handed for my taste. Never looking anyone in the eye. Last time we met, the poor thing was shaking from head to toe. Just like Genebra's pinscher—the dog is gone, too, it seems."

Ariadne frowned. She took a silk nightgown from the floor and followed the trail of clothes to another room. Augusto walked behind her, muttering that Genebra must have left in a hurry, but she stopped paying attention when she reached the bathroom. On the sink were Erik's old glasses, along with a double-edged razor blade, shaving cream, and a blue toothbrush across from Genebra's things.

"I think I found Erik's room," announced Augusto, and she went after him.

The room was similar to the master bedroom, but she could see Erik everywhere. There were books on the desk, on the nightstands, and on the floor; the bed had been made like he always did, with the pillow on top of the sheets; there was an empty coffee cup on the rug, and crumpled toffee wrappers. She touched a white dress shirt neatly folded on the chair and checked the collar: as she expected, there was an *E* and a *Y* embroidered on it, like on all of his clothes.

"I don't know what we're searching for," said Augusto, stepping on a cockroach. "Do you?"

"Any clue to where they went."

On the desk were two books on obstetrics and several

letters. Some were unopened, but most had been read and folded many times. *I can help you if you help ME*, said one of them, signed by R. *I wouldn't ask you if I wasn't desperate. I have nowhere else to go!* Ariadne checked the sender's address, but the envelope was blank. *I've been following the instructions in your last letter, but my blood pressure is still high. Do you think this will affect the baby?*

PLEASE MEET ME, read another letter. Ariadne ripped open one of the envelopes to see an unread note, and the content startled her. *It's your choice, really, to keep ignoring me like this. If my child dies, and you know that she might, it's your fault. MURDERER.* In another, the writer went further: *I can tell him where you are. I can just say: take a look at Genebra's house! And you're gone. Easy, just like that.*

"Augusto, do you know any pregnant guls?"

"Rafaela's the only one I can think of. Why?" Augusto skimmed through the letters with a grave face. "It does sound like something she would say. And her husband has contacts."

"What kind of people are they?"

"The happy couple?" mocked Augusto. "Not the good kind. Then again, which gul is?"

"What about you and Quaint? Are you bad?"

He scratched his chin, his stocky fingers lost inside his beard.

"It's something I always ask myself. Am *I* good? Can I be good? Is there any point in trying?" Augusto shook the curtains of the bed, and a cloud of dust surrounded him. "I flatter myself time after time, reassuring my troubled mind that I only eat the vile. And they *are* vile, oh yes. Quaint and I have a taste for the truly rotten. I don't question my judgment of their character, but what does that make me? Those idiots patrolling the streets at night also believe they are taking justice into their own hands. At the end of the day, I still think I'm right, and I want to do what I can."

"You have to eat," Ariadne pointed out. "Guls can only process human meat. The death squads don't have any excuse for selling their own."

"Yes, well, but why only humans? Why would nature do that to us? That's what keeps ringing in my head."

"Koalas only eat certain types of eucalyptus, which is poisonous to most animals. You're not special."

"I just fail to see the purpose of this existence. Are we here to eventually disappear, like we're already doing? There are fewer of us every century, and there are more elders dying than children conceived. Are we your only predators? We're already failing at that, and I don't like the sound of it either. Are we supposed to keep hoarding and living lavishly, until we're no longer here?"

Ariadne placed some letters inside her purse. The skin of her arms had been made so carefully that it even had greenish veins underneath the yellow undertone, slightly darker around the knuckles and elbows, matching the ones around her eyes, her neck, her inner thighs.

"I could tell you the same thing. To you, I'm prey. I'm aware of it every second of the day. I know, too, that my existence as a person, no matter how well-intended, is flawed. I have to consume what victimizes others—clothes, food, technology—to survive, at least in the world we know right now," she said. "Keep doing what you can."

"Still, it's frustrating. I can't understand Quaint, who chooses to live side by side with humans, or Genebra, who eats her decrepit friends when they tell her they're ready to die. Then I look at you and wonder how you can live with us and treat our health, knowing what we do—or worse, what we *want* to do."

"I know what to expect from guls." Ariadne massaged her upper arms, feeling a hint of pain. "Knowing how bad you can be makes me feel safe, because I *know.* I can't say the same about my kind."

The last room they entered was the kitchen. It had no fridge or stove, but there were expired packages of biscuits on the table and an empty milk carton near the trash. The pinscher, they found, was heavily decayed, and Ariadne would have guessed he had died locked up and hungry if the flooring had not been damaged by a bullet.

When they finished searching the apartment, Ariadne and Augusto returned to Cabaré. *I'll stay until Quaint comes back*, he assured her without a smile, *for your safety.* Augusto scowled whenever Friedrich and Lena walked near them, never interacting but always close, sniffing the air around her. *Some people can't see a human on their own without thinking they're in a restaurant* . . . At about six o'clock, Quaint descended the staircase and thanked Augusto, and a taxi took them to the hotel.

"The receptionist said there are no other guests on our floor," said Quaint when they were alone in the mirrored elevator. "They made it gul-only after the curfew law. Humans don't know, of course, they think it's merely being refurbished, but I'm pleased that we can talk freely here. Mind accompanying me to the pool?"

"Pool?"

"I need some fresh air." Quaint led the way down the corridor, removing his jacket and rolling up the sleeves of his shirt. "I'm feeling a little suffocated."

The pool he referred to was not the main one she had seen through the window, but a more private one located on the gul-exclusive floor. As he said, there was no one else there, not even clerks or maids, only empty sun loungers.

A light breeze brushed her face, and Ariadne leaned against the screen panels to look at Copacabana beach. The ocean was already dark, as was the bottom of the pool, and the potted plants adorning the terrace ruffled with the wind. Quaint undid his tie with a sigh.

"You look like you discovered something." Ariadne stared at the black water. The last time she had been to a pool was almost twenty years ago, at the age of thirteen, and she felt a childlike urge to jump into it. *There's no need for a swimsuit,* someone had encouraged her back then, open hand on her tiny back. *No one can see you from here.* Instead of jumping, she knelt in front of the pool and touched the surface with her fingertips.

"Have you?"

"Maybe."

"Ladies first."

Ariadne sat on the floor, taking the letters from her purse to give them to Quaint. It took him a few seconds to realize what they were about, but when he understood, he began to read eagerly. While Quaint walked around the pool, holding the letters up to his face, she took off one of her flats and touched the water. Ariadne submerged one toe, feeling the warmth of the pool, then her entire foot.

Behind her, Quaint huffed with irritation and crumpled one of the envelopes in his fist.

"Spectacular. Simply spectacular."

"Augusto thinks the letters were written by someone called Rafaela."

"Oh, they were *definitely* written by Rafaela." Quaint took a deep breath, his figure becoming harder and harder to discern as night fell.

"Who is she?"

"A self-centered, unhinged gul who managed to find a husband even worse than herself, and now they're reproducing." Quaint folded the letters and put them carefully inside her purse, crouching by her side. "Her husband, Damião, is so odious that I have to restrain myself from jumping onto his neck every time we meet. Hopefully, we won't have to deal with him at any point. Only Rafaela."

The lower part of her leggings was already wet, and she glanced at him from the corner of her eye. Quaint was little more than a shadow, recognizable only by the outline of his hair, nose, lips, chin, neck.

"What about you?" asked Ariadne. "Did you find anything?"

"Some government officials were looking for Erik last year. The band said they were all half-eaten humans."

"Half-eaten?"

"I suppose they meant the amputees that appear on TV."

Half-eaten, she thought dryly, her leg going up and down in the water. His expression softened, and he pointed at the pool with his chin.

"You can go in if you wish."

Ariadne thought of several excuses that ranged from not having appropriate clothes to not feeling like it, but again none of them felt right. *I can't, I'm half-eaten*, her mind whispered maliciously, and she shook her head. *Worse than eaten*, she corrected herself, *ugly*.

"Don't look." Ariadne removed her leggings, wriggling them out from under the dress, to submerge both legs. It had been a while, she realized, since she had seen either the night sky without a roof above her head or her own body with someone next to her. Quaint chuckled when she elbowed him playfully to cover his eyes, and he raised one hand to his face, obeying the request. Ariadne left the piece of clothing rolled up by her side and turned to him. "Quaint?"

"Yes?"

"The apartment looked like they left in a hurry. At first, I thought they were escaping from something, but we found Genebra's dog in the kitchen with signs that he had been shot. The doorman also told us they left with a few visitors, but he didn't recognize any of them."

"Huh."

"Aren't you worried?"

"The more I know, the more confident I am that we'll find them alive."

Ariadne bit her lower lip, tasting blood where she had bitten it during the nightmare.

"Is this related to what happened in 1972?"

"That's . . ."

"If it is," insisted Ariadne, "you need to tell me."

He looked at her for a few seconds, and she realized that it really was dark. The hotel had forgotten to illuminate the pool, and the moon and stars were hidden by heavy clouds. Still, there was almost no distance between them, and she could feel his eyes considering her, his fangs clenching inside his jaw, his body tensing at the thought of sharing whatever had happened so many decades ago.

After a long moment, Quaint spoke:

"For many years, especially between the fifties and sixties, Erik and I were very close. We even lived together for a while in Argentina, then a couple of years in Brazil, on and off. By 1971, our initial affection cooled down irreparably because of his newest scientific curiosities, but we remained good friends." Quaint touched the water as well, his ringed fingers whirling in the pool. "In 1972, he calls me to his new house in Vitória. We're having a conversation, and he tells me he's going to get something to eat in the kitchen. The memory becomes foggy after that. I wake up the following day, strapped to a dental chair. I'm confused, but I can't move. My left hand is searing with pain. He sedates me again. This goes on for a week or two, until he decides it's time to release me."

The nightmare burned inside her throat. Ten pairs of teeth, bloody gloves, a dental chair. And the yellow house that might not have been yellow at all, a tongue going down her throat, and raspy, disgusting words: *I won't ever tire of you, you're staying here until you die . . .*

Ariadne couldn't answer. Whatever Erik had done was too far from the man she knew and too close to the part of her mind she refused to touch. She made an effort to nod to show she was paying attention, but her eyes were lost somewhere in the water.

"Erik used me to get a gul's genetic material and observe how our regeneration process works under duress." Quaint lifted his hand, pointing at the base of his little finger, and droplets of water fell down his wrist. Ariadne touched the faded scar over his knuckle, feeling the subtle difference in skin. "I imagine he excused himself by saying that it was not my dominant hand, that it was just a little finger, and I was sedated during the entire process. I only felt glimpses of pain when he severed it over and over and over again."

"But why? Why would he . . . ?"

"Erik gulified himself, and the result is that he has an enhanced lifespan and a taste for red meat. Nothing beyond that. Otherwise, he's human and eats like one of you."

Ariadne remembered how Erik had eaten twice as much as her, but, naive as she had been, she had thought it was because he was an adult man. *Erik, that's not rare, that's raw,* she had told him many times, but Erik had just laughed like a misbehaving child. *You're gonna get sick one of these days . . .*

Her hand lingered on Quaint's, hovering over the peony, and he didn't move away.

"I don't understand why you're trying to help him."

"My foolish heart knows no reason. I forgave him, or perhaps I felt avenged when he never grew back the foot he lost to test his own experiment." The lines on the back of his hand were stiff, the salience of his veins evident under the tattoos. "I don't know if he deserves my forgiveness, but Erik has never gulified anyone but himself. I'm sure he was kind to you, as he was kind to me on many different occasions, but this is also part of who he is."

The lights around the pool turned on, and Ariadne blinked, unaccustomed to the artificial illumination. She hurried to get up, pulling the dress down to cover her thighs as she was hit by a sudden wave of shame. Quaint grabbed her purse and stood up as well.

"What now?" asked Ariadne, turning around so he wouldn't see her face.

"Now we get you something to eat. Tomorrow, we find Rafaela."

This time, they went to the Italian restaurant downstairs, fuller than the one they'd previously been to, and they stuck to small talk. Quaint insisted she could order anything—*I love watching others try what I will never eat*—and even made jokes with the waitress, as if they had not talked about his own amputation moments before: *Oh, no, it's only for her, I have been tragically cursed with so many food allergies that you wouldn't believe . . .*

Back in the suite, the red roses had been arranged in a crystal vase and placed on the coffee table. Ariadne took a long bath after they retreated to their respective rooms, trying to tame the unruly thoughts in her head. *Don't make that face, we're the same!* Erik had said, taking off his shoe and sock to reveal the prosthesis. His model was older than hers, something he had developed before they met. *Why don't you make one like this for yourself?* Ariadne had tapped the titanium. *Why? I'm just an old man.* Erik had laughed it off. *I'd rather focus on you any day . . .*

Ariadne put on one of Erik's old shirts and went into the empty living room. She sat on the rug and started to search the journals until she found the one from 1972.

I have been considering the alternatives. Ideally, I would need a willing partner, but I don't think I will find one among the guls. The only person who could be convinced is Genebra (she would say yes, I'm sure she would, especially if I explained that I could help many others if this works) . . . But I can't imagine hurting her.

"Can't sleep?" Quaint stood at the door, and she raised her chin to look at him. His hair was down and wet, and he walked barefoot toward her.

"I'm trying to find something about this gulification process, because there are surely higher-ups interested in doing it," said Ariadne. "I want to know what to expect, and why thcy need human body parts for the process."

Quaint sat cross-legged on the floor and opened one of the journals.

"Do you mind if I read with you?"

"Be my guest."

I have been checking my muscular strength, and there have been some improvements, but nothing too remarkable, said one of the post-experiment notes, together with kilogram numbers from the grip dynamometer: 45, 50, 60, 65. *My teeth have also remained the same, but that was to be expected*, said another, together with folded realistic drawings of gul and human dentition. *Some relevant changes in my appetite: I have been craving meat in unreasonable quantities, thankfully not human. I have tried what was left of my foot, but found it too repulsive to keep in my stomach.*

Quaint stretched his neck to read over her shoulder. *Big mistake to have been so arrogant as to think my foot would grow back like theirs do!* Ariadne read several reports Erik had made of the changes, most of them inconclusive. *Quaint woke up a few hours ago; tried to bite me right away. He was always prone to overreaction*, read one of the entries that made her feel sick to her stomach. *Good news: while he did manage to break my nose, it seems that I have some enhanced regeneration, and might recover quickly.*

"I should have eaten him when I had the chance," snarled Quaint. He seemed ashamed of having voiced the thought, but Ariadne smiled, forgetting about the journal, the nightmare, Cabaré. The absurdity of it made her laugh, and she covered her mouth to hide a chuckle. "And you laugh at it!"

Quaint closed the journal and threw it on the pile of notebooks, a mischievous grin appearing on his face as Ariadne tittered.

"I'm sorry—it's just—the idea of it, for some reason . . ." The smile hurt her cheeks. Quaint laughed, too, and she wished that was it: it was all a joke, what happened to him, what happened to her, what Erik had done. "This is so surreal. The Erik I knew was the opposite."

"You seem to have met a gentler side of him."

"I guess I did." Ariadne took one of the earlier journals distractedly, leafing through the pages.

Yesterday, Quaint took me to the Juliette, an underground bar for goules. Genebra, the lovely Portuguese lady who was in his Montparnasse home the other Monday, said she could take us there at eight, and so she did. They were both so finely dressed when the car arrived that I tried to rush back to the boardinghouse immediately, with the intent of never going out again, but that seemed to amuse them further. The Juliette . . .

"Maybe not this one," said Quaint, covering the rest of the page with one hand. "I would have to check what he wrote first."

"Ashamed of something, I see."

"Not ashamed, just . . ." Quaint took another notebook, and she panicked when she saw it was the journal that came after the one she had read the previous day. "Oh, you're here! '*Ariadne is especially fascinated with gul dentition. We spent the entire night discussing her questions regarding anatomy, and I must say she had the funniest—and wittiest—questions. She was not tired in the morning (oh, to be young . . .), and she got to perform her first tooth extraction. Terebê approved of it: said she is quicker and more delicate than m—*'"

Ariadne almost jumped over him to take the journal from his hand, her cheeks ablaze. One of the corners of his mouth curled up, and his long arm held the notebook in the air, far from her reach.

"Not that one."

"Fair enough." Quaint returned the open journal. Erik had drawn her on the page: a messy black bob cut a little above her jaw, tired eyes, and an unfitting girlishness in her cold expression. *She has the blackest eyes!* said a little note near her face. "Too bad. You look sweet there."

"We both have our secrets." Ariadne got up with the notebook in her hands, and offered a quick smile. "Good night, Quaint."

Later, she dreamed she was back at Erik's office, and all his belongings were still there. Everything was in its place: the desk, the cabinet, the shelves, everything but him. Ariadne sat down, feeling the leather cover of one of his Russian books, and stopped reading when she felt someone breathing behind her, blowing warm air against her neck.

A man grasped her by the jaw and forced her to stand. *Quaint*, she tried to say, but he opened a mouth full of teeth. *Qianyi.*

Quaint ignored her pleas. Instead, he smelled her, brushing fangs against her skin and ripping her shirt like it was made of paper. His nails left pink marks on her breasts, and his teeth sank into the smooth flesh of her neck, drawing blood that dripped down her torso in crooked lines. He pushed himself between her legs, biting again. *Qianyi*, she said, not knowing what it meant. Quaint was eating her, but she didn't feel pain; she wanted him inside of her, again, again, slamming her body against the desk. A hairpin fell, metal clinking against the flooring, and his nails scratched her hips.

The bites moved on to her belly, the muscles of her inner thighs, the softness of her groin. Quaint climbed over her, face dripping with red, and she hugged his waist with her legs, her real legs.

Ariadne woke up, and the name was still trapped on her lips: *Qianyi.*

IV

Labyrinthine

Light filtered through the stained glass windows, casting multiple colors on the hallway's runner rug. Quaint tried to open another parlor, but it was locked again, like much of the second story of Cabaré. The repetitive failure reminded Ariadne of the yellow house of her dreams, a house with almost no corridors, only room after room after room, many of them identical, making her feel like she was entering the same place over and over again.

Augusto stopped in front of the imperial staircase after minutes of fruitless search.

"I think Damião's hiding from you. Someone must have told him you were around, and he went back to his place with his tail between his legs."

"Why is he hiding from Quaint, in particular?"

"Why indeed." Quaint reclined his shoulder against the bronze statue of a woman holding a candelabrum. "Let's say

I have ruined one of his businesses in the past. And let's also say that he's afraid of being eaten."

Augusto crossed his arms. "Maybe they're upstairs."

"You two stay here," Quaint started to say, but Augusto interrupted him with an incredulous laugh.

"She won't ever talk to you alone!"

"They are not to be trusted around a human," stressed Quaint.

"What can dogs do, bark?" Augusto shook his head dismissively. "They won't attack her, Quaint. Not here. Not if we're around."

"I'll wait in the library." Ariadne touched the enamel pin on her chest that was given to human attendees who frequented the second and third stories. "Isn't this supposed to show I'm not food?"

"Yes, *but* . . ."

"Then go."

After they headed upstairs, Ariadne walked aimlessly, following the long and antique runner rug. Despite being emptier, the upper rooms felt suffocating; if the first story were an open mouth, the second would have been a clenching throat, and the third the lower esophagus, just above the cardia of the stomach. The placid old lady she'd seen the day before was there, walking with her elderly gul, and the pair entered one of the parlors. The woman made the sign of the cross, and Ariadne couldn't help but notice that, today, she didn't wear a lapel pin.

In any other building, the library would have been a comforting place, but in Cabaré, there was a certain eeriness to the beauty of the next room she entered. The walls had been recently repainted, the ceiling had frescoes, the shelves were tall and organized, and there were oil paintings and bronze busts throughout the entire room.

Ariadne admired the pictures, and stopped in front of a large framed photograph of the members of Cabaré, dated 1963.

About twenty people stood in a large ballroom. Some of them were guls she had already seen, like the German couple, or the little boy with tourmaline rings, a robust toddler at the time. Genebra was right in the middle, recognizable by the straight waistline of her flapper dress, her lean physique, and her bobbed hair. Augusto smiled by her side, and he had changed considerably: he was much thinner in the picture, his hair had been braided into neat cornrows, and he only had a shade of a beard, but his dark skin now had no more lines than it had in the sixties.

On the far left, she recognized Erik, who had to have been around forty by then. His light hair was styled to the side, and he wore round tortoiseshell glasses and raised a glass of champagne in the air. Quaint was by his side, wearing a mod suit, one of his arms resting on Erik's shoulder, the other hand holding a cigar. The two looked like they had just shared a particularly funny joke and were doing their best to suppress their laughter, and Ariadne found herself saddened by the thought.

She observed other guls she had never seen before, and her eyes stopped on a familiar figure on the other side. A heavy man, muscular and bigger than all the others, with his hands stuck inside the pockets of his pinstripe pants. The sleeves of his shirt were rolled up, revealing the profuse hair that covered his arms, and the dark stubble did not hide the thick fangs that forced his jaw outward.

Everything disappeared at the sight of him.

Ariadne could no longer remember where she was, which journals she had read, what all those books around her were, who Quaint was and what his face looked like. Not even

Erik existed anymore. In her mind, she was inside the yellow house, strapped, tied, locked; she was bound to the chair, to the bed, to the floor; she was there, and no one else existed but the man keeping her inside.

Here, she told herself, feeling like the floor was trembling under her feet. *I'm here.* Ariadne blinked several times, staggering toward the corridor in the hopes of feeling some fresh air, but the club felt bigger and emptier than before. The throat closed around her.

"Rafaela? Are you coming?"

Ariadne raised her head when she heard the name, the pool of gastric acid no longer drooling from the organ walls and floor, back to a regular club of plaster, cement, wood. A gaunt man with chalk-white skin stood in front of her. His features formed a mental sketch somewhere in her memory, in a place she thought forgotten, rearranging him until she could understand the picture: a pencil mustache under a pointy nose, an outmoded suit, a cane in one hand, a top hat in the other. A strange-looking man who came sometimes, the afternoon's historical telenovela playing in the background. *He looks like one of the characters*, she would childishly think, looking at actors on the TV.

Huh was all Ariadne managed to say. Her fingers trembled, and there she was again: the very image of a broken doll, no arms, no legs, nothing left. The alarms went off in her head. Part of her, beastly and inconsequential, wanted to grab the gul by the neck and squeeze, squeeze, and squeeze, like they had done to her.

Damião was also paralyzed. All traces of color had vanished from his already pale face, and his eyes, sunken and rat-brown, consumed her from head to toe. They stayed far too long on her face, recreating her younger self, then wandered over her body, over the mature plumpness of her curves, making it very clear that she was a grown woman, not a child. Finally, he stopped at the limbs that should no longer exist, and before she could say anything, he ran. Damião fled toward the staircase, faster than she thought possible, and Ariadne ran after him.

What would she say, if she reached him? There was nothing to be said. Would she ask him to confirm the deluge of images inside her mind? Question if he was sorry, if he had ever regretted it, even for a day?

Ariadne faltered. Her legs no longer worked. She leaned against the wall, watching Damião meet a young woman on the stairs and rush past her, pulling her by the arm. *No,* she thought, then *yes.* Only the woman was not leaving with him, no matter how many times he called her—*Rafaela, come now, Rafaela! Don't be like this!*—she was marching toward Ariadne with a vicious look on her face.

Rafaela was tall and skinny, making her protruding belly even more visible under her tight turquoise dress. Her loose curls enveloped the skin of her bare shoulders, of a similar tawny color to her hair, and her thin features twisted in a grimace. To a human, she looked like she was around thirty, like Ariadne herself, but she couldn't have been fewer than three centuries old. Bitterly, Ariadne thought that a woman like her would have been the perfect companion for a man like Quaint, both beautiful and well-dressed, tailor-made for such a refined place.

Rafaela flashed a smile full of teeth when she stopped in front of her.

"The man you're accosting is my husband," she said, soft and melodious. Rafaela cornered her against one of the walls, towering over her. "What business do you have with him?"

"Your husband." Ariadne processed the words. "Poor thing."

"What did you say?"

"That I pity you," Ariadne said, now louder. "That's what I said."

How easy it was, to shut down all the feelings that flooded her head, seeping even from the most locked corners. Ariadne had done it before, opening an imaginary trunk and shoving the memories inside of it until her head was blank. After closing it, she could not remember almost any detail of what she had hidden there, but, like a rotting corpse, its blood would sometimes leak, reminding her there was something deeply wrong inside. Again, she pushed the images of the yellow house inside the trunk, and faced the other woman.

"You should avoid stress in your condition." Ariadne offered a cruel smile, wondering if Rafaela knew what her husband did and who he befriended, or if she would care about any of it. "By your size alone, I'd say you're almost reaching your third year, aren't you?"

Rafaela's fangs appeared under her maroon lipstick, and a guttural growl came from her throat.

"Who are you here with?"

"Quaint brought me. Heard your husband is not very fond of him."

"Of course it had to be one of Quaint's humans to ruin my day, like one wasn't enough!" Rafaela huffed, and a curl flew off her face. "He told you, didn't he?"

"Told me what?"

"Don't play dumb now." She clutched Ariadne's face, the

gul's long acrylic nails sinking into her cheeks. "Of course Quaint bragged about killing Minotauro. Do you think that means you're better than me? Stick to your man, and I'll stick to mine. Quaint might pretend he's oh-so-good, but he's still alive, isn't he? Alive, healthy, and eating like the rest of us."

Minotauro. The name reverberated in her bones. It took her back to that world where nothing existed. What did Quaint have to do with Minotauro? The words were tangled in her head: Erik, Quaint, Minotauro, herself. Rafaela claimed he had killed Minotauro, and Ariadne knew that she had to leave the club now. Had Quaint helped Erik save her? *He doesn't know who I am*, she thought, shocked by the realization. *He doesn't know Erik took me with him.*

"Keep your petty fights to yourself," said Ariadne, her throat going dry. "Just tell me where Erik is, and we're done with this conversation."

Rafaela blanched. "I don't know where— Why would *I* know?!"

Ariadne took one of the letters from her purse and pushed it against Rafaela's breastbone.

"Skip the bullshit. Where is Erik?"

"I don't know." Rafaela held her belly with her two hands, and Ariadne grasped her wrist before she could scurry away. "I have nothing to do with this."

"It's a high-risk pregnancy," insisted Ariadne. "You need help."

"I have to go, right now. I have to go!"

Ariadne squeezed her wrist harder, knowing it was nothing compared to a gul's strength.

"You need a doctor, Rafaela."

Before she could continue, Rafaela slapped her arm away and fled in the same direction her husband had gone. Quaint was already descending the stairs and calling her name, but Rafaela growled instinctively, more animal than human.

I must look like hell. The thought felt distant, her mind drifting away. *Ariadne* must have, considering the look of concern in Quaint's face, but she couldn't move or speak. Instead, she just stared at the place those people had been, hearing his steps coming closer.

"Ariadne?"

She was not there.

Ariadne was not even her name.

In the yellow house, she was not a person, just a thing to be used. Minotauro always told her she was buying her time—each year that passed, the reason changed. At seven, because her seriousness intrigued him. He hated crying, and she didn't cry, not even once. At eight, he claimed she was the prettiest, and that all the other children paled in comparison. At nine, after she hid in the basement, hoping to escape when he left, he decided she was too smart for her own good. *I'm not a cruel man,* Minotauro had said, dragging her by the neck up the stairs. Her feet rattled against each step. *To show you how good I can be, I'll give you three chances, and if you manage to find your way out of here, I won't even stop you if you win.*

At ten, she planned attempt number one. She knew he could smell her if she hid, so she waited until he visited one of the other kids, and left through the window of his bedroom. *No noise,* she told herself, climbing down the cat's claw vines. *No noise.* She sprained her ankle when she fell on the grass, but it didn't matter, because she was almost out of there. If she ran, if she could run . . . She swallowed the pain, but made it only a few houses away, where a neighbor kindly brought her back to the house to treat the calcaneal fracture she'd suffered during the fall.

At eleven came attempt number two. She had been reading his books, searching through the medication he kept in the surgery room, reading all the leaflets of all the boxes. The skin on her arms had bruises from fangs scattered all over it, and she made a shallow cut near one of them, filling a single cup with blood. *And a bit of Rohypnol*, she told herself, taking the cup to bed. *Don't bite me*, she purred, smiling sweetly when the blood stained his lips, kissing his sturdy neck. *I'm in a lot of pain today, please, please.*

That time, she almost made it. She lay by his side until he was fully unconscious, took money from his wallet, and left through the front door. The problem, she realized, was that she didn't know where she was. She didn't know the streets, the neighborhoods, or where a bus could take her. She didn't know how to explain what Minotauro was. She couldn't even recall where she'd lived before. The last thing she remembered was staying the whole day in a park, watching as people went by. Then, she got up and returned from where she came.

At twelve, one last failure. By that point, she had lost all hope that he would tire of her. All the other children were disposed of after a year or two, and she had expected him to do the same when her body started to change. It had been changing for the past few years, first subtly, then faster and faster. *Here*, he cooed every day, taking a tiny pill from a pink blister pack and caressing her belly.

Pregnancies, said Minotauro, were a risky business at her age. He knew of a few cases of men who had impregnated human females, and neither mother nor child lived much after it. The babies could not eat by themselves, and only a few women carried their pregnancies to term. *Maybe in the future*, he had said, *but I don't want you to die, not now, not now.*

She waited for the perfect day. For months, she had been paying attention to his conversations to learn more about the city. She still didn't know how to ask for help, but she had been saving the money she took discreetly from his clothes, and her bag included a few clothes and extra food. *Never again*, she told herself, walking out of the yellow house.

And what are you *doing here?* an amused voice asked behind her back. The street had been empty a second before, but there was a man there, a man with a top hat. She tried to run to the other side as fast as she could, but when she looked up, he was already in front of her eyes. He grabbed her by the neck to drag her back. *To me, you're just a mouse struggling in a trap.*

The memories were dissolved by someone's warmth.

Ariadne looked to her side. Quaint held her hand, his skin hot and real, his long fingers covering hers. *Follow the thread*, Erik had reminded her, and her mind reorganized itself, like a store returning every product to its respective shelf. They were not in the yellow house. They were inside a taxi, going to a white hotel. Damião and Minotauro were gone, and so were the weeping children she refused to think of. She was not a little girl, she was a woman, and the man by her side was Quaint.

The taxi stopped in front of the entrance.

"Can you get up?" Quaint asked gently. Ariadne blinked, recognizing his face: his straight black hair, his tan skin, his round glasses, the curve of his nose, his lips, his chin.

"My legs are weak," she admitted, barely recognizing her own voice. Ariadne couldn't remember what had happened after she talked to Rafaela, and could only feel grateful for his patience so far. "Sorry."

"I'm worried about you. Can we talk now?"

"In the room."

Quaint and Ariadne sat across from each other in the living room of the suite, one on each sofa. He probably expected an explanation and a report of her encounter with Rafaela. She, on the other hand, was slowly discerning the shape of her flats, the black pantyhose covering her legs, the tulip skirt, the cardigan, the blouse.

"If anything happened when I was upstairs . . ."

"Something happened, I guess." Ariadne looked at Erik's calligraphy in one of the journals. *Q. called me cruel,* read an entry. *He thinks death is the most merciful gift those children could receive, a swift, revering, painless death. Maybe he's right. But when I saw her, stable, responsive, the last one remaining in a mass grave, I knew I had to give her a chance. A chance to look back, with autonomy, and decide if life is worth living, after all. A question I still don't know how to answer, myself. That's why I didn't tell him I took her with me.* "I'm not sure what to do with it because it also involves you."

"I don't know what Rafaela told you, but that woman's husband was involved with a very dangerous gul."

"Minotauro?"

Quaint faced the closed window. The sky was dark, and a streetlight flickered outside. Soon, there would be the high-pitched whistle announcing curfew, and not even the distant chatter from nearby restaurants would be heard anymore.

"What did she say about him?"

"Rafaela? Nothing interesting." Ariadne wanted to look firm, serious, indifferent, but her ungrateful body betrayed her, it always did. "What do *you* have to say?"

Quaint took an embellished cigarette case from the inner pocket of his jacket. "Do you mind?"

"Go ahead."

The cigarette hung from his incisors, and he flicked open a silver lighter with his thumb.

"I should have stopped smoking years ago," muttered Quaint, more to himself than to her. He dragged on the cigarette, his chest puffing under the shirt. "He was a member of Cabaré until—well, until his death. We called him Minotauro because of his looks. Massive man, bull-like. Used to work as a surgeon in the past."

"A surgeon."

"Another doctor, yes. He would spend a decade or so working in one city, then move to another before his employers could suspect anything. Sometimes, he also treated guls."

"Were you friends?"

"No, I never trusted him," said Quaint. "There was something about Minotauro that made my skin crawl. The way he spoke about others, about humans in particular . . . In this, Erik and I agreed."

"The others didn't?"

"Even Genebra and Augusto thought we were imagining things." He paused to find an ashtray, but ended up dropping the ashes on a napkin. "Said we were bickering about politics, like we simply resented him for treating us as representatives of the Eastern Bloc. Like the problem was him saying that communists had no place in Brazil, instead of the clues that he was involved in something questionable."

"With Damião."

"See, Ariadne, it's shameful to admit this, but most guls have preferences in their eating habits. My father only ate eunuchs. Genebra went from elderly Portuguese duchesses to equally elderly modern friends. Others like certain body parts. The list goes on." His lips curled in disgust. "Minotauro and Damião never had any qualms admitting that they preferred human children. Now, eating children is not exactly taboo among guls. It's mostly the kind of thing we agree you should not look *for*."

"But the others didn't care when they did?"

"It could have been just boasting. Damião, in particular, is very fast, but physically weak. A vulture. Some men like to prove themselves, especially in the company of one another. But then Erik heard them speak about a 'restaurant' they owned. This is where the situation becomes disturbing."

Ariadne nodded.

"We envisioned this plan where we would go to Minotauro's house when he least expected it. Damião was out of the country. My mother always said that the big ones fall the hardest, and I thought that, maybe, I could take him down on my own if he attacked us." Quaint let out a strangled laugh. "We thought they were just *eating* children. I didn't expect what we were going to find there. Never, never, never . . ."

"Did you kill him?"

Ariadne wanted to get up to take off his glasses just to see the look in his eyes when he said yes or no. More than anything, she needed a confession and a reason, and she hoped that the right answer would soothe her heart.

The smoke escaped from the corner of his lips as more ashes fell on the napkin. "I did."

"Why?"

"Don't be scared of me, please. I would never . . ."

"Why?"

"Because I couldn't accept that someone like him existed. Because I was afraid of what he could keep doing if he stayed alive. Because there is no punishment for guls. Because I still can't stand to think of what I saw."

Ariadne processed the words slowly, thinking: *I want to leave. I want to stay. I want to leave . . .*

"Erik said something about it, didn't he?" Quaint massaged his temples. "He never agreed with what I did, if that's what you're wondering, but he didn't stop me either. I was consumed by my rage, and even though he knew what I would do, he closed the door, waited outside, and pretended not to hear a thing."

Ariadne could imagine that scene. The two men in the photograph, dressed in their fine suits, one entering the master bedroom on the upper floor of the yellow house, the other locking the door and closing his eyes. It was just like Erik, wasn't it?

Ariadne got up and looked at Quaint, feeling like she was seeing him for the first time. His dark hair had fallen out of its pompadour, his wide shoulders were stiff with tension, his mouth was projected forward to keep the cigarette in place. When Ariadne didn't answer, Quaint raised his chin, and she saw his eyes, too, black like hers.

"That's what I wanted to know." Ariadne began unbuttoning her cardigan. "How I would feel about it."

"What?"

"If I would be glad or if I would hate it." She dropped the cardigan onto the floor, her arms visible under the cap sleeves of her blouse. "If I would feel avenged. If I would be sad. I guess I don't feel any of those things."

"Ariadne . . . ?"

"I can't do it faster." Ariadne extended her arm, finding the line where the synthetic fiber touched her scarred stump. She unrolled the skin carefully, exposing the bionic arm underneath. "You have to take it off slowly, or the sensors might break."

His eyes were fixed on her, and Quaint was no longer a predator, but a fellow person. Vulnerable, uncertain, confused—all feelings she had as well. Ariadne walked up to him, feeling no shame when her fingers trembled and he held her hand, putting out the cigarette to help her remove the soft layer covering her limbs.

"Is it strange? That I'm not satisfied by his death?" Ariadne continued under his mesmerized gaze. "I didn't want you, of all people, to carry this weight. And, at the same time, childishly, selfishly . . . I wanted someone to end things. To be angry for me. To care."

Ariadne bent over to pull down her pantyhose, peeling the tights and the synthetic skin of her legs. When she finished, she was only wearing the skirt and the blouse, exposing the robotic limbs willingly for the first time.

"Funny to think I resented whoever killed him for not killing me as well. I don't resent you anymore." Ariadne seized Quaint's glasses by the bridge, closing the arms and leaving them on top of one of the journals. "Why the face? You'd eventually find out. Erik would tell you, so what's the use in hiding?"

Ariadne knew the answer to her own question: it was the same reason that made her wake up earlier in the day, flushed and gasping for air, with the images of the dream still drilled into her head. It was the kind of reason that made her hate herself, that took her to a dangerous mental space, one where she missed what Minotauro did because at least he wanted her; at least in his eyes, she was something that could exist, a marionette coming alive under her puppeteer's touch.

Usually, that would be sufficient to fill her with dread and disgust, but this time, she felt an almost ethereal relief, like Minotauro had never existed in the first place.

It was as if she had stood in front of him many times and done the same thing, recognizing that expression, that person, that moment. If she closed her eyes, Ariadne would see Quaint when he was not yet Quaint, but a smiling boy called by another name. First, with long hair tied in a bun and smoky quartz glasses, swearing they would always be together. Second, his chest against her then-flat chest, lying on a wooden floor, saying they should run away. Third, with a hasty glance from afar, betraying the kindness of a long-forgotten husband.

If she opened her eyes again, the present Quaint would be there, but it was still the same man.

"I'm at a loss," he admitted.

Ariadne smiled.

"I like leaving guls speechless. Might make it a habit."

Quaint smiled back and touched her face.

Ariadne rubbed her cheek against his hand, feeling the lines of his palm, the cold metal of the rings, the subtle salience of the peony tattoo on the back. She kissed the tips of each finger, the nails, the knuckles, the little white scar. She looked at him to see if he would reject her, and when he didn't, Ariadne covered his index and middle fingers with her mouth.

A low sound came from the bottom of his throat. His nails touched the roof of her mouth, and her lips went up and down, leaving a trail of saliva on his skin. She looked down, an old fear still fluttering in her stomach:

"Am I disgusting?"

Am I disgusting? The same question, a different time. Erik had held her by the shoulders, gently stopping her after an awkward attempt at a kiss. His shaking hands patted her neck, like saying sorry, like it was hard to do that, like he found her too vile to bear. She had never been so ashamed of being so ugly, so despicable, so insignificant. *No one will ever want me again.* Not with that body, not with that past. Only Minotauro could have wanted something like her. *I know you're trying to hurt yourself,* Erik had said, covering her with his own coat. He had explained that while he was flattered, he was too old, and she was still recovering. *Don't cry, don't cry . . .*

"Nothing about you is disgusting." Quaint wrapped his arms around her narrow waist, burying his face in her belly. "I just need to know if you're doing this to hurt yourself."

"I'll hurt myself if I pretend I don't want you inside of me right now." Ariadne ran her fingers through his hair, dissolving what was left of his hairstyle. The shame returned, poison spreading through her veins, but this time it was much harder to walk away. "I'm sorry. I thought . . ."

"You thought right." Quaint lifted her like she weighed nothing, and Ariadne placed her knees on the sofa, sitting on his thighs. "I'm not denying you in any way. I just don't want to take advantage of your pain."

Her body trembled with anticipation, feeling the fabric of her skirt lifting itself around the width of her hips. *I want, I want, I want,* and everything else disappeared under his touch. There was no yellow house or the memories hidden inside of it; there was no Minotauro or the abrasions left by his hands; there was no clinic, no Erik or the thoughts that had haunted her every day since she woke up. Then, and just then, there was only him and her.

V

A Mouse in a Trap

The colors of the dream were muted, but the rope around her neck was tight. Not her neck, no, another person's neck: taller, bonier, with an Adam's apple going up and down. Her fidgety fingers adjusted the knot, the stool under her feet trembled, and she breathed heavily, sweat dripping from her pointy chin. It all had been too much. Since her—his—desertion, since before, even, since he was conceived, and he couldn't even focus on the phantoms of good news coming from the Allied troops.

I should've been saving lives, he thought, and everything in that sad, impersonal room felt laconic and gray. It was evident now how little he was, how little all of them were, how even survival was pointless—nothing could fix what he had already lost. How did he go from being on the run to landing in a tiny boardinghouse in France? *France, of all places . . .*

He was about to kick the stool when a stranger opened the door.

"Oh, my," said the man. "You're not German, are you?"

Erik blinked. The man scratched his own chin, thoughtful, his tattooed hand appearing under the sleeve of a gabardine topcoat.

"I don't understand," Erik mumbled, hand still grabbing the rope. "I don't understand a single thing you say."

The man smiled and shifted to a functional Russian, eyeing the red cross satchel on the bed.

"Soviet? Lucky you. Now, take that thing off of your neck! The Allies have just reached Paris, haven't you heard?"

The room changed to a car. A Bentley Mark VI, in fact, information Ariadne would never have known otherwise. Her chest fluttered, flat under a comfortable shirt tucked inside her pants. *His* pants.

"I think he's nervous," said Quaint by his side, playing with the suspenders on Erik's shoulder. "We're not going to devour you, Doctor. Yet."

"That's what *you* say," Erik replied with an anxious little laugh. The woman on the other side laughed as well, and the hairs on his neck bristled, feeling her breath. "I'm not entirely certain about . . ."

"It's so sweet that you've been pure all this time . . ." Genebra's hand slipped to his stomach, and Quaint undid his tie. Heat twisted his underbelly, and Erik shifted in his seat. "Not even a brothel? Not even once? Twenty-six is not that young, is it? By human standards."

"No, I guess it's not very young." Erik gulped when the man by his side kissed his bare neck, tongue and teeth tracing the line of his hyoid bone and feeling blood pumping inside his jugular, threatening to sink in. "Careful with the teeth, yes?"

Genebra laughed heartily, leaving lipstick marks on his chin. "You were right, Quaint, he's very amusing . . ."

Now they were in the middle of a ballroom, and his heart was drumming inside his chest. Erik adjusted the tortoiseshell glasses on his thin nose and took a deep breath, facing a large gul.

"Listen, we're not accusing you of anything. It was just an honest question."

"*I* am accusing," Quaint added sharply, and Erik had to control an irritated sigh.

"I'm trying to talk here, Quaint. Let's all be calm and polite, yes?"

"And what are you accusing me of?" Minotauro cracked the knuckles of his right hand, fist against palm. The hand alone could crush his skull, maybe even Quaint's. "Say it to my face."

"I'll break it down for you." Erik took a sip of wine and met Minotauro's dark brown eyes. "What do you mean, exactly, when you claim veal is best? Because, well, I was thinking, see, unlike you, I *have* tried veal, and I have tried regular beef, but you can't possibly know the difference, because your body only turns the protein found in human meat into amino acids. Which implies—"

"I'm sure he understood what it implies," Quaint interrupted him.

Minotauro twisted his lips, the severe prognathism caused by his lower canines turning his smile into a grimace.

"Quaint takes everything too seriously, don't you think, Erik?" Minotauro poured more wine into Erik's glass.

"Sometimes, yes," replied Erik, oblivious to the irony. He glanced at Quaint, at the vein popping under the collar of his shirt, at the stiffness of his strong jaw. "But I think his concern is valid."

"Quaint thinks I hate humans. Too bad, because I think we all have much to learn from him. Lately, I've even been thinking of doing the same thing he did, get myself a nice human wife, although the one I'm thinking of is not quite ripe yet. Do you recommend it, Quaint? A litter full of half-breeds?"

Their reactions were too fast. Quaint and Minotauro roared, and someone yelped, urging them to stop from the other side of the ballroom. Erik grasped Quaint by the arm before he was too unreasonable, and the gul's sheer strength threw them both to the floor. Augusto held Quaint in a headlock, and Damião and Friedrich jumped to contain Minotauro. The larger man fought under them, a boar struggling against his captors.

"Don't listen to him," Erik whispered as they hurried back to their feet. Quaint growled at him as well, wild, feral, so unlike the Quaint he knew.

"What if I do, human-fucker?" Minotauro shoved Friedrich aside and bared his fangs. His roar reverberated in the ballroom, and Erik felt himself shaking at the sound, paralyzed, no more than weak, helpless prey. "What can you do about it?"

His words mingled with the sound of a maid knocking on the door. Ariadne opened her eyes. The images of the dream dissolved, a blur of crumpled ties, bared fangs, and animal growls. *I often have dreams of lives that are not even mine*, Erik had said once. She wondered if she, too, was more sensitive with guls around her, or if it was all a projection, her head patching pieces of the journal together even in her sleep.

The faint smell of cigarettes clung to the sheets, and Ariadne remembered where she was. Not with the noose around her neck, not with Minotauro, but lying in Quaint's arms. She touched his chest, her index finger following the lines of the birds drawn on his skin, the blackness of it turned into a greenish hue.

"Good morning." Quaint put his phone aside, and Ariadne caught a glimpse of the news on the screen: *The president made an official statement during a video conference to his followers, but he has not been seen in public since . . .* "You looked like you were having the most disquieted dream."

"I think you were in it." Ariadne kissed his chest, trying to memorize the lines of the wings, his collarbone, the prominence of his neck. "What's this one supposed to represent?"

"Not much," said Quaint. "Two friends once drew it for me in a letter. It was not my favorite artwork of either, or their best, but it was the only one that I owned after their deaths."

"Artist friends?"

"One was a most gifted sculptor and painter from a prominent local family. Met him on my first journey to Europe, when I stopped by Florence." His hand guided hers through the tattoos, holding her index finger from image to image. "The other was his model, apprentice, servant, lover. The lines blurred at the time. A sweet thing, but what a temper! Drew very prettily, too, though his art is all but gone."

"Except in you," said Ariadne.

"Except in me," Quaint agreed. "I'm a walking memorial."

"You seem to have had a very busy life." Ariadne crawled over him to sit on his lap, still feeling the past night inside of her. Now, she could see where the tattoos covered him: his neck, his arms, his chest, the fronts of his thighs. She had seen glimpses of the ones on his back, but his stomach, feet, and lower legs were clean. "The opposite of me."

"Only sometimes. Then, I was young and discovering many things about the world and myself. What I liked, what I disliked, what my beliefs were . . ." Quaint buried his fingers in the folded skin of her hips, keeping her close with a strong grip. "I learned plenty, but the agitation of youth was a little too much for me. I, too, prefer a quiet life."

They stayed in bed for a long while, and she wished they never had to leave. It was pointless: Erik and Genebra were still missing, Rafaela was out of their range, and Quaint . . . Ariadne shook her head. Right now, she could pretend there was no past or future, only the Ariadne who smiled when he brought her lunch, or the Ariadne who kissed him again when she was finished, or the Ariadne who pressed against him in the shower.

Later in the evening, they tried to go to Cabaré again, but neither Damião nor Rafaela were around. The same happened the following day, but this time they questioned other guls. *I think it's because of last time*, drawled Ubirajara, pointing at the ceiling with a bored look. *You were quite the animal, Quaint, what did you expect?* Rosa tittered from the sofa: *I'm sort of glad that Minotauro is gone, he gave me chills.* Then, the German couple in the smoking room: *Yes, Damião talked to me*, Friedrich conceded. *I don't think he'll show his face again unless you're out of town, boy.*

His wife, Lena, had another opinion, claiming they would certainly appear at the ball. *Rafaela loves to parade her pregnancy, Damião will stupidly agree, thinking you won't be there, and they're both vain enough to think it's safe,* she said, looking insistently at Ariadne. A thin smile appeared on Lena's face. *Now, Quaint, I'm expecting that if you decide to appear, you won't behave like you did last time . . .*

"We have to go to the ball."

"I don't feel comfortable taking you there," said Quaint. "Not after the things you told me."

"Will they eat me?"

"I would never allow it." Quaint looked at the invitation that had been given to every gul at the entrance, scanning the lines of the dress code that instructed members to wear black tie only in the permitted colors. "Augusto is also rather fond of you, which surprised me, because he only ever felt contempt for Erik."

"So they won't eat me, *but* they might eat other humans."

Quaint sighed. "Yes, if there are other humans there, you can assume they will be eaten. Not in public; Cabaré has specific rooms for that. At the parties I have attended, it was considered distasteful to bring unwilling humans, but still. No. We won't go."

"I can convince Rafaela. I *know* I can." Ariadne sat on his leg, and looked at the invitation. There was a mention of a plus-one, and an additional note: *Bring your own meal.* Again, she thought of the club as a digestive tract: the window teeth, the hard palate ceiling, the carpet tongue, the imperial staircase uvula. Then, ascending through the pharynx half-landings, crossing the fibromuscular walls of the esophagus, was the stomach, lined with fine decorative tissue and bathed in acid, all arranged in perfect menace.

She held him by the cheeks. "I want them to know who I am."

"Ariadne . . ."

"I trust you. Against my better judgment, against my instincts, I trust you. Can you trust me, too?"

"Then we'll have to get some clothes."

The ball was scheduled to start on Friday, but they only planned to attend the opening night, as guls, in their strange atemporality, could spend days partying like the world had stopped for their pleasure.

In the morning, she woke up alone in the suite. Ariadne knew that Quaint hardly slept, but he had been gracious enough to spend the entire evening with her in bed during the past few nights. According to him, outside of his hibernation period, which could take a few years or even a decade, he only took a few sporadic naps. He wasn't in the living room either, but he'd left a garment bag with his ironed suit, and a red box with her name on it.

For the few hours he was out, Ariadne prepared herself. At the drugstore, she bought painkillers and candy bars, and her eyes wandered to the condoms in the aisle across from the clerk. *Maybe I should . . .* The thought left as soon as it came; she wasn't even sure if it would make any difference, as Erik had never mentioned hybrid children, and Minotauro lied more often than he told the truth. Back at the hotel, she charged both her phone and her limbs, and packed everything she would need in her purse: a pill organizer, a wallet, snacks, carfentanil.

I'm not scared of them, she told herself, hoping that, if she repeated the words enough times, they would become true.

"I'm sorry it took me so long," said Quaint when he arrived. He began undressing after he closed the door, kicking off his shoes and unbuttoning the cuffs of his shirt. "I had to get the clothes, talk to Augusto, leave our names on the guest list, discuss certain safety terms . . . It doesn't matter. I need to take a shower."

"Go ahead." Ariadne helped him with his tie and belt, and followed him into the bathroom. Quaint entered the shower almost right away, leaving his glasses on the sink. "Why are you nervous?"

"At the last ball I attended, my behavior was less than stellar."

The flash of an unknown memory crossed her mind. Quaint, curled lips revealing potent fangs; Erik, rushing to stop him to no avail; Minotauro, squirming free of the people trying to contain him. Ariadne played with the old-fashioned straight razor inside the toiletry bag, opening it and closing it with her fingers.

"You should take it," said Quaint, his voice muffled by the sound of water. "We're most sensitive in the eyes."

"I won't stab anyone, if that's what you're suggesting."

"Just as a precaution."

Ariadne smirked, standing in front of the door of the shower.

"You *really* are nervous."

"Are you enjoying my pain, miss?"

"I'm amused that you're more concerned than I am."

Quaint got out of the shower, drying his hair with a towel. Water pooled on the floor under his feet, and she stepped aside.

"Speaking of which . . . Have you tried on the dress I bought?"

"Just to see if it would fit," answered Ariadne. "I'm surprised you knew my size."

"I have an excellent tactile memory, it seems." Quaint wiggled his fingers in the air before finding the hair dryer, the pomade, and the comb. "At least I'll have something to look forward to tonight."

Ariadne went to her own room to bathe. She was glad that Quaint had chosen simple clothes: a little black cocktail dress with T-bar flats of the same color, a detail that made her smile, as she could hardly take the discomfort of wearing heels. In another woman, a form-fitting outfit would have looked fine, beautiful even, but there was not much to save in her case. Not with that face, not with that figure.

Ariadne looked in the mirror. The thin straps of her dress showed her bionic limbs, and the fabric ended just above her knees, exposing the prosthesis without the synthetic skin. Indeed, there was nothing she could do about her features, but there was something to be done about the rest.

The car dropped them in front of Cabaré at eight thirty. Quaint had already made a deal with a human driver hired by the club to take them back to the hotel after curfew, a privilege that guls had acquired in a discreet deal with the government. They just needed to be quiet about it, and identify themselves as club members if they were stopped by the police. The exterior lights illuminated the garden, and a distant melody could be heard from outside.

"I must admit I'm glad to have you with me," said Quaint, taking her hand and entwining their fingers together. "Pathetic, isn't it? You're the human, and I'm the one searching for the comfort of your presence."

"What are you scared of?" Ariadne asked. There were shadows dancing on the grass and muffled laughter from the upper floors.

"Of being unreasonable again." Quaint touched the back

of her hand as delicately as he would have if there'd been frail skin to break, not the black and metallic lines of the limbs. "Of being alone in a place where they would accept the unacceptable than act against it."

Ariadne straightened the peak lapel of his wine-colored tuxedo, and looked up to see his face.

"I'd rather see you angry at the right thing than laughing at it."

"Let's pray that won't be necessary tonight." Quaint opened the door. "I was hoping you would dance with me."

"You should find a partner your size. I'll make you look ridiculous."

"Nonsense!" Quaint laughed, heading upstairs. He greeted a human butler with a bow of the head, but the eyes of the man were fixed on Ariadne's limbs. "I always had a soft spot for petite frames. Took after my father, I guess!"

Two waiters descended the other flights of the staircase, and Ariadne couldn't help but feel the warm mouth of a beast around them, the mucosal tissue of the gingiva wallpaper, rosy and smooth, the lit chandeliers blinking like the enamel of teeth.

"Quaint." She squeezed Quaint's fingers with one hand and the chain of her clutch bag with the other. "*I'm* scared."

"I won't let anyone hurt you."

Ariadne hid her face in his arm. In her mind, she could still feel Minotauro over her, fangs sprouting from his lower lips, dense hair covering his arms, chest, and face, a low growl coming from the bottom of his throat. *He's dead*, she told herself, *and if he wasn't, Quaint . . .*

"Quaint, Ariadne!" a third voice called them. Ariadne lifted her head to see the short and brawny gul who had just opened the door of the ballroom. "I was starting to think you would leave me alone here."

"Of course we wouldn't," replied Ariadne, smoothing her voice to a neutral tone. "Good evening, Augusto."

Augusto kissed the back of her prosthesis.

"Good evening to you, too, my lady. I see that you are dressed to impress, or may I say undressed?" Augusto looked at her robotic parts, and his expression became stiffer than before. Despite his polite smile, she could see there was something in the sight of her limbs that unnerved him; maybe he had expected her amputation to have been just the arm he had seen, not such an extensive part of her body. Augusto patted Quaint's shoulder before she could overthink it. "Rafaela is here, but Damião is nowhere to be seen."

"Perfect."

The ballroom felt familiar, like she had seen it a long time ago, or in a half-forgotten dream. The walls were taller than the rest of the mansion, the room spacious, and a small band played music next to the window. If she just focused on the clothes, the jazz, and the dancing, she would have thought the place was trapped in the thirties or forties, but if she looked closely, she found some smartphones on the round tables, together with a few modern garments here and there. Ubirajara, the slender singer who was often downstairs, wore a long evening gown with glittering sequins, and sang slow songs with a husky voice.

If she wished hard enough, Ariadne could have thought it was a party like any other, but she couldn't, and it wasn't. All the tables had crystal bowls with raw meat ribs organized like refined appetizers, as well as mortars with crushed bone. Friedrich sometimes dipped his thumb in the bone dust and licked it, laughing as he talked to a quiet Anzol.

And, of course, there were the looks. Quick glances and unwavering stares, gawking at her body like they had never seen anything like it—anything like *her.* Ariadne pressed her lips together, wanting to hide behind Quaint's wide back, but she stared back. When she did, she realized there was no hunger in the countless eyes around her, but fear, discomfort, alarm. Some guls retreated when she walked near them, but the looks continued no matter where she went.

Minotauro, someone said. *He ate her, but she survived . . .*

"A bunch of blabbermouths, us guls," Augusto commented disdainfully by her side. "Have you told anyone else? News travels fast around here."

"I haven't," answered Quaint. "I guess his fame precedes him."

Minotauro, the voices kept whispering. *Minotauro.*

"I don't care if they know." Ariadne tried to search for Rafaela in the crowd, and found her on the other side, chatting with the mother of the little boy. If Rafaela had noticed their presence, she did a good job of pretending not to. "It makes no difference to me."

"If you want my opinion, you two should mingle before you approach Rafaela, and look as vapid as she is." Augusto adjusted the bow tie of his midnight-blue tuxedo. "Talk. Laugh. Invite Ariadne to dance, or I will. Just play the game and act nice."

"Augusto is right." Quaint unfurrowed his brow and offered a courtly smile. "Shall we?"

Quaint took her to where the other guests were dancing, and she rested her cheek against his chest. Erik had done the same, many years ago, playing music on his outdated record player and bowing to ask her for a dance. *I don't know*, she had stuttered, *I never . . .* Erik's laughter was crystalline. *Then let me teach you!* He took one of her hands and placed the other on his shoulder, hunching down to match her size. *I have been complimented a few times on my skill at the Charleston and the tango, but the waltz has never been my strongest suit.* Erik had led her through the kitchen as Leonard Cohen sang on the record. *One foot here, the other foot there, you're doing great . . .*

If she closed her eyes, Ariadne could ignore that there were others in the ballroom, scraping meat and grinding bones with their sturdy teeth. She just had to follow Quaint's light steps and slow dance, his hand resting on her lower back.

But if she opened them again, she would see the humans. An elderly man guided to a private room. A young couple undressing in a corner. They looked at her, too, a wild expression crossing the girl's face when she realized what Ariadne was: a half-eaten human dancing with a gul. The man shook his head, defeated, and entered a parlor, but the woman stayed there.

Ariadne closed her eyes again.

"I don't know why they look at me like they've never seen a human interacting with a gul before," she muttered, looking up to see his face. "Haven't you brought Erik here? Haven't you danced with him, too?"

Quaint's fingers stiffened around her waist.

"I have."

"I can't imagine that. I know he can dance, but he's so awkward . . ." Ariadne smiled against his chest. "Not that I am much better."

Quaint pulled her by the neck to kiss her mouth, and fragments of words were lost in her throat: *no, you're lovely, so lovely . . .* At times, she thought he wasn't speaking Portuguese anymore, but she could still understand, and the only thing that broke the spell was the human woman she could still see from the corner of her eye.

Across the room, the girl covered her chest with her blouse, nauseated at the sight of them. Ariadne reciprocated the revulsion. The idea that those people *chose* to be there disgusted her and made her want to shake their shoulders to ask *why, why, why?* If only she had had the chance, sometime in the past . . .

Another woman moved next to the human, walking past her as if she did not exist, the tail of her dress flapping behind her.

"Rafaela's moving," Ariadne said against his lips. "I'll talk to her."

Ariadne hurried to the other side of the ballroom. She dodged dancing couples and avoided the tables, almost jumping back when someone touched her shoulder. A sickly-looking waiter offered his bitten arm, purple marks going from his wrist to his elbow. She remembered having the same bruises: *the finest wine,* Minotauro had boasted, tongue running through the holes left by his tusks, *enough to make anyone drunk.*

"Thirsty, ma'am?"

Ariadne knew he had been drugged by his unfocused eyes and slurred speech. That, and to withstand the pain—the horrid feeling of fangs plunging into skin and flesh. *For a girl who can be so cold, so unfeeling, so mean,* Minotauro had said, holding her limp wrist in the air and offering it to Damião, *she tastes rather sweet.*

"No, thank you." Ariadne thought of saying something else, but it was pointless. If he hadn't noticed she could not possibly have been a gul, he was not conscious enough to hold a conversation.

To focus, she tried to remember why she was there—*Erik needs me*—and kept repeating it until she reached the restroom.

All the stalls were open, and Rafaela stood in front of one of the mirrors, fixing her makeup. She hadn't noticed her presence yet, and Ariadne closed the door behind her.

"Hello again."

Rafaela's bored expression turned into shock when she looked at her, eyes growing wide as Ariadne came closer and leaned against the wall near her. Rafaela grimaced, then pointed at her limbs with her chin.

"Did he eat them?"

Ariadne touched her own exposed arms. She remembered the way Erik had described the eaten and the dead in his journals, but had no recollection of the moment of her release. *Seven children, some as young as six, the oldest one no more than thirteen or fourteen; used, their bodies half devoured and decomposing—I wish I could forget.*

"Minotauro?" Ariadne felt a wicked satisfaction in seeing her squirm.

The oldest girl without arms and legs must have been his favorite, Erik had written. *Despite the amputations, she's healthy, well-fed, and has been kept alive, unlike the others. I don't want to imagine for how long . . .*

"He didn't," said Ariadne. "He cut them off so I would never run away again."

Rafaela narrowed her brown eyes. The empire silhouette of her gown highlighted her heavy belly, and the high heels made her look even taller, but Ariadne was no longer scared.

"I didn't see Minotauro very often," said Rafaela. "Only at parties and such. I wouldn't know."

"I don't care. I'm here to see how you're doing. Are you happy?" Ariadne pointed to her belly. "Your husband must love children."

Rafaela let out an angry noise, a mix between a shriek and a growl.

"He didn't— Damião didn't participate in any . . . !"

"Didn't he?" Ariadne asked no one in particular. "Calm down. Stress isn't good for the baby."

"Haven't you three done enough harm?" Rafaela hugged herself protectively. "Yes, Minotauro overdid it, but I had nothing to do with that! What do you want from me?"

"I have an offer to make."

"Offer?"

"It's ironic, if you think about it." Ariadne walked around her, seeing both of their figures in the mirror. Rafaela, lean, elegant, with a healthy glow in her skin and her salmon gown almost reaching the floor, and herself, short, unsightly, dressed in black. "That your husband caused all of this. If they hadn't done what they did, Quaint would never have killed Minotauro. If he hadn't killed Minotauro, you never would have asked Erik to help you, because you would have had a doctor by your side. If Erik had not disappeared because of you, I wouldn't be here."

Rafaela breathed audibly, her chin trembling.

"It doesn't matter. None of that matters. I don't need . . ."

"I read your letters," continued Ariadne. "Your mother died from a maternal hypertensive disorder, and now your blood pressure is high, too. That's why you're so desperate."

Rafaela punched one of the mirrors with her closed fist, and the shards fell to the sink and floor.

Ariadne didn't flinch.

"This is not an offer!" Her hand bled, but she didn't seem to mind, removing pieces of glass while grinding her teeth.

"You're terrorizing me, that's what you're doing. You horrible, horrible woman."

"Don't interrupt me," snapped Ariadne. If Rafaela thought any of this would scare her after everything that had ever been done to her, she was very, very wrong. "Without all of this, Erik would have never trained me. I would never have become a doctor, like him, who can treat a gul, like you."

Blood stained Rafaela's light dress, but the tissue of her hand was already closing the cuts.

"*You*'re a doctor?"

"Rafaela. Think about whether it's worth raising your baby with a father like this. Think, too, about if you want to live the last year of your life pregnant, remembering what I just told you. Imagining what could—what *will*—happen to you. Imagining, if you die, what would happen to your child . . . If your imagination runs wild, who knows what could happen to your health?"

"You're threatening me."

"Swear now that your useless, pathetic husband will never harm anyone again, and that you will take us to where Erik and Genebra are." Ariadne offered her hand, a discreet smile appearing in the corners of her lips. "In exchange, I will stay by your side. I will care for you, and we will deliver this child together safely."

Rafaela stood immobile in front of her open hand. She covered her mouth, and let out a strangled laugh.

"This is crazy."

"Crazier than marrying him? I doubt it."

"I need to think," said Rafaela, opening the door. Ariadne ran after her. "I don't know, it's too . . ."

They were back in the ballroom, and Rafaela looked

around, as if trying to find somewhere safe. Ariadne grabbed her arm, pulling her down to speak close to her ear.

"This is your last chance."

Before Rafaela could push her away, two raised voices and a wave of scandalized whispers made them turn around. *Again*, someone said, looking at the entrance. *They're doing it again*. Ariadne glanced at Rafaela, who had stopped because of the tumult, her long neck stretched to see above other people's heads. On the other side, Augusto was talking to the unsettled human girl she had seen before, covering her with his dinner jacket. Ubirajara still sang, oblivious to the fight, and Quaint grasped Damião by the shoulder.

". . . won't do anything tonight. I just want to know where Erik is."

Damião stared at the hand grabbing his arm with disdain.

"And why would I know? I don't like him any better than I like you."

"Play nice," warned Quaint, but his grip was strong enough to twist Damião's arm slightly. "I know Rafaela is involved. Where is he?"

The two women exchanged glances, silently agreeing to move toward the fight. This time, it was Rafaela who clasped her hand, dragging her through the crowd.

"I don't question my wife about her business." Damião dusted the sleeve of his double-breasted frock coat like it had been tainted. "Go bother her instead. Or don't, because that would just upset her, and there's nothing sadder than a dead child, don't you think?"

Quaint's nostrils flared, and Ariadne walked faster. Her free hand fumbled inside her purse, searching for a familiar shape.

"That's low even for you."

"Ignore him," Augusto said, a few meters from them. "The trash won't take itself out, but they sure like to talk, don't they?"

Under the chandelier, the purple veins under Damião's eyes were more visible, and fangs appeared when he curled his lips, a rabid dog gaining momentum. Ariadne froze when their eyes met. In his presence, she was still the little girl who watched as they took turns biting her arms, blood gushing until she was dizzy and weak. The only thing tying her to the present was the pain caused by Rafaela's clawing fingers on the back of her hand.

"It's you," gasped Damião. "You're little—"

"Don't say that name." Ariadne's voice almost faltered. In a second, he was in front of her, bizarrely fast, nauseatingly close. Damião's brown eyes scanned her from head to toe, and he made a thoughtful sound.

"At first, I wasn't sure because you shaved your head, and because . . ." He spoke in a low and hurried voice, his spidery fingers reaching out to her face, trying to trace the absence of black hair, but Ariadne flinched, ducking. Behind Damião, Quaint and Augusto roared, shouting for him to stay back. "Now I can see it's really you."

"Me," Ariadne repeated laconically. She searched for the veterinary automatic syringe, one hand discreetly buried inside her purse, checking the liquid bottle and touching the handle.

Rafaela's fingers slipped from hers and fell to her side. The other woman seemed in shock, gawking at their interaction in disbelief.

"Come, now—I wasn't the one who hurt you, remember?" urged Damião when he saw his wife's face. He rubbed his cane with a gloved hand. "They're upset because they think I was the one who did it, but if you tell them the truth . . ."

"The truth?" Ariadne couldn't register the people around them. When she blinked, the walls turned yellow, and she was be trapped in the old house again. "*You* were the one who took me there in the first place."

"I did you a *favor*, do you think you were any better where I found you? Do you think things would have turned out any differently for you?" Damião whispered frantically, his pale face awash in outrage. "The people who gave you to me were no kinder than Minotauro was. They were just human."

Ariadne stared at his shoes. In her heart, she knew it was true, and that the apathy with which she had accepted everything was just a sign of it. Minotauro's compliments were a constant reminder that her old life was no better than her new one: *She never cries, she never complains, she was born for it.*

"That's no excuse for doing the things you did, and yet you did them anyway," replied Ariadne with a hollow voice. The walls around them were no longer yellow, and when she looked at him, there was little left of the terrifying outline of the man in the top hat. It was just a man, and a weak, tedious one at that. "That's the only truth I'll tell."

For the first time since they had arrived, Rafaela moved, jolting her husband by the lapel of his coat. Her growls were even louder than the men's.

"And what exactly did you do? *Huh?*"

"Nothing! I never touched her, I swear." Damião glanced at her, as if expecting Ariadne to back him up. "When he was finished with the kids, I ate them. That was our deal."

"Whatever makes you sleep better at night." Ariadne let out an angry laugh and turned to a livid Rafaela. "And whatever you want to believe."

"*Enough.* You have no right to talk to her—" Quaint pulled Damião by the neck, forcing him away from Ariadne like he was pulling a dog by the leash. "I will ask one more time: where are they?"

"Even if I knew, I would never tell you," snarled Damião, his voice turning feral as he became more agitated. A smile crept onto his face. "A friend for a friend."

His hat fell to the floor, and he tried to bite Quaint, who dodged and punched him in the face. The sound of fist against nose made Ariadne's stomach churn. Thick drops of blood fell on Damião's white tie, and he groaned, curling in on himself, one hand slipping inside his frock coat. Before anyone could react, he jumped on Quaint.

Damião was swift: avoiding a second punch, neck bending sideways right under Quaint's wrist, lock-blade knife snapping open under his thumb. The blade cracked one of the dark lenses of Quaint's glasses, and he stumbled back, covering his face. Rivulets of blood dripped from Quaint's left eye to his neck, soaking the collar of his shirt, like tangles of red veins.

"Quaint!" Ariadne and Augusto screamed. Damião charged again, but this time she ran toward him, grabbing him by the collar of his shirt, throwing her arms around his head from behind, trying to claw his eyes.

Sharp teeth invaded the metal of her prosthesis, and Ariadne gasped. The pain lasted only until the sensors broke, making her entire arm go cold. She took the syringe with the other hand and slammed it against his neck, pumping tranquilizers into his jugular vein as she pushed the bitten arm against his jaws.

"You—" Damião tumbled into her arms, convulsing and looking at her with bewilderment.

Ariadne held him as he fell to the floor, lowering his heavy body with the same care she would have given a sack of sand, seeing herself reflected in his eyes.

"To me, you're just a mouse struggling in a trap," she said, and Damião passed out.

VI

Dr. Erik Yurkov

Ariadne cleaned Quaint's forehead with a gauze sponge. The cut went from his brow to his left eyelid, and had caused some damage to his eyeball, but most of the blood loss had occurred when the blade reached the supraorbital artery. His sclera was still scarlet, but the dilated pupil that leaked into the umber brown of his iris was returning to its normal round shape; as expected, he wouldn't need sutures. Despite his dizziness, the tissue was regenerating fast, stopping the blood and stitching threads of skin together.

I can walk, Quaint had said as they left Cabaré. He had looked paler and thinner as she guided him to the elevator, and collapsed in the living room of the suite after a minute or two. Ariadne removed his rings, the dinner jacket, the black tie, and his shoes, laying him against the sofa seat. After checking the wound, she asked the gul clerk if he could buy her a few things from the drugstore, even though Quaint's body would do most of the work.

Quaint slept with his head on her lap, his shallow breathing the only reason she knew he was alive, and Ariadne washed the sweat off his face and the thick dried blood from his hair. She looked at the only ring left, the one with the braid, and read its inscription: DIED 12 OCT 1912. Sometimes, she took a quick nap, but the images of the past night kept haunting her: Damião, slipping from her fingers into unconsciousness, his vile words, the bitten arms of the waiters.

"Shh," hushed Ariadne whenever his body tensed, caressing his head with the hand that could still feel. The other prosthesis was completely numb, but its movements were mildly functional.

To distract herself, she read Erik's journals, opening one from 1966.

> *There is always this ghost behind him, this elusive love that represents an ideal of perfection, and we fought again about it. I'm not the jealous kind, I told him, I don't care who he has been with during his long, long life. I just think it makes him have high standards for how people should be, feel, or behave, comparing them to this first girl, who died tragically but was ever faithful to him and he to her.*
>
> *I am not trying to compete with her (or anyone! God forbid . . .), but I can be a little selfish, and a little rude, and a little careless, and love is not the only fuel for my soul. He says I lack empathy, though I disagree, and that I value ideas more than people, which might be true. I do think I've been getting more and more carried away with my research since I started to dabble in other fields. I also fear that a piece broke inside of me when we met—something special, irreparable, intimate—and I can't help but blame Quaint for the mangled humanity I have left.*

Ariadne placed Quaint's head carefully on the pillow and moved to the floor, her cheek close to his arm. Another entry detailed a week in Beijing, where Erik had visited the National Library, the ruins of the Old Summer Palace, and the National Art Museum. *Q. didn't want to visit the Forbidden City again with me, a sentiment his mother shares. Too bad!*

There was a letter that had been ripped from the notebook, then folded and glued in again. *I said all of this without thinking, but we have already talked it out,* Erik wrote on the outside. Inside, it read:

> *I think it's pointless to keep insisting on this fruitless endeavor. You are right. We have nothing in common, and we're both dissatisfied most of the time. Our tastes don't match. Our tempers clash. Our morals are in constant conflict. We don't even agree in bed. I do love your company, and our conversations, and your face, but now more than ever I think: what are we even doing together?*
>
> *At times, I fear that you search for pain. That you're addicted to the tragedy that is loving humans. You find one of us to seduce, and they're all fascinated by you (who wouldn't be?), but they—WE—are simply too feeble, too ephemeral, too mortal. Then we die, and you suffer, until you find a new human to do the same with. I don't want to be part of this, of your fixation with sadness and loss; it deeply disturbs me, in fact.*

FUCK YOU, ERIK appeared in the handwriting of somebody else in capital letters. *You don't understand (never have and never will) ANYTHING about me.*

Ariadne put the journal aside. Was she also part of this

fixation? She tottered toward the bathroom, facing herself. The fabric of the dress was crumpled; the spaghetti straps were hanging from her shoulders, exposing the lace of her black bra. What an unsightly thing she was, so human, so weak, so frail. She had been an ugly child when she was taken to the yellow house, she had grown into an ugly teenager by the time Erik rescued her, and she would continue to be ugly for the rest of her life.

Tears blurred her sight. Ariadne had cried all she had to cry after Quaint went to sleep, grieving every second she'd spent inside Cabaré. *I never hurt her*, or whatever Damião had said. *Tell them the truth.* If Erik had been compassionate, she would not have had to hear any of that. If he had smothered her instead of taking her home, she would not have grown up alone and rejected, stuffing those memories somewhere she didn't have to see them all the time. Maybe, like he said, she would stand a chance in her next life.

"Ariadne?"

Quaint was behind her, a thick red scar covering his left eye, and she took a few seconds to turn around, trying to compose herself.

"Are you feeling better?"

"The pain is mostly gone." Quaint unbuttoned his stained white shirt, throwing it near the towels. "I thought I heard you calling me."

Ariadne helped Quaint with his clothes, and he washed his face in the sink, scrubbing more dried blood from his hair. The water ran rust red, almost brown, and he looked at his own hands.

"Thank you for taking the rings off for me," Quaint said, bending down to continue washing his face. "Although I'm curious to know why you left this one on."

"You never take this one off." Ariadne dried a few more tears when he wasn't looking. "Isn't it your wife's?"

Quaint rubbed the crystal of the ring with a towel, wiping it gently. His left eye was still closed, and drops of water ran down his neck and the lines of his back.

"No, this one is hers." The rings were stuffed in one of the pockets of his pants, and he lined them up on the porcelain of the sink. She picked up the discreet golden ring with a simple skeleton drawn in black enamel, engraved with the name FANNY and a date: JANUARY 1917.

"You must have loved her a lot."

"Oh, I did." Quaint smiled when Ariadne put the rings back onto his fingers one by one. "We were the greatest of friends."

"Friends."

"We were better friends than we were husband and wife, but that doesn't mean we didn't cherish our life together," said Quaint. "We just failed at the romance. It happens, sometimes. With some people more than with others."

Ariadne looked down, tears pooling in her eyes again. Her throat tightened and the bathroom became a wet haze. In her mind, she wished she had died in the yellow house, and never had the chance to meet Erik or Quaint. Maybe it was just the shock from the previous night, but it didn't matter when she felt about to collapse.

"Were you crying all this time?" Quaint held her by the face, his tone kind and soothing, but she shook her head. *I don't want kindness*, she wanted to say. *I want you to use me, I want you to fuck me, I want . . .*

"No, no," Ariadne mumbled, trying to cover her face. "I wasn't."

"Don't be ashamed in front of me." Quaint pulled her to his chest, kissing the shadow of her hairline, her small forehead, her nose, her lips. "Cry if you feel like crying."

"Please, don't pity me," murmured Ariadne. She stood on her tiptoes to deepen the kiss, hugging his neck, hoping he would not push her away. Quaint didn't. "I don't want you to see me as a helpless child. I don't want to be trapped there forever. This is not all I am, I promise it's not what I am . . ."

One of his hands fell to her back, and he bent down to pick her up by the back of the thighs and lift her up, their bodies pressed together like they needed to be closer, closer, closer. Ariadne circled his neck, hugging him as soft sobs escaped her throat. She didn't recognize her voice, high-pitched and pathetic, and when she saw their reflection in the mirror, she didn't recognize her face either. Her lips were red and swollen, her dark eyes glittered, her cheeks were stained with tears. Yet Quaint looked as gentle as he did before, with no trace of judgment or irritation in his open eye.

"I know it's not," Quaint said. "I shouldn't have left you alone after what happened, but I'm here now."

Ariadne traced the white line of fibrous tissue that went from his brow to his lid. The wound already looked old, not yet faded, but a hypertrophic scar starting to regress. She guessed the only thing keeping him from being fully healed was the corneal injury, as the eye was an organ that guls struggled to regenerate. Ariadne tangled her fingers in his black hair, recognizing each strand, feeling the coarseness of the undercut and each ridge of his skull.

Quaint took her to the bed, and she pulled him to lie over her.

"Touch me," Ariadne pleaded, guiding him between her legs. If he didn't, she would still be the girl who knew only Minotauro's hands. "I beg you to touch me."

Quaint caught her tears with his lower lip, tracing her face with his fingers like she had done with his. Eyelashes, nose, mouth, tongue, chin. Her dress was lifted to her waist, and his hand caressed her slowly, almost asking if he could, if he should, if she really wanted this. *Yes.* Ariadne nodded. *Yes, please.* She didn't know how to explain that she would never ask for something she didn't want ever again in her life, not anymore, not with him.

Quaint pulled down the straps of her bra and buried his face in her chest, kissing the skin between prosthesis and arm, her breasts, her belly, her inner legs. "*Be happy, Ariadne mine*," he quoted, and she swore she had heard the same poem many years ago, recited from another mouth. His visible eye reflected the little light coming from outside, the glow in the pupil caused by the tapetum lucidum behind his retina giving him an unreal aura, half human, half beast.

After they finished, Quaint curled behind her, making her feel small between his arms. She closed her eyes, lulled by his steady breathing, and slipped a hand under his.

"Quaint." Her legs were trembling, and the skin of her thighs was wet and sticky, but she didn't move away from him. "Have you ever seen a hybrid?"

Quaint nuzzled the back of her head. "Are you worried?"

"Minotauro used to threaten me with it," whispered Ariadne, about to drift away.

"Once, I met a little girl who needed human flesh, but couldn't digest it. She died at a very young age of what is now known as kuru." Quaint squeezed her, every centimeter of him against her, like he, too, needed the safety, warmth, comfort. "Her teeth were too brittle, her skin too thin, her limbs malformed." He showed her his open palm, then closed his fist around Ariadne's hand, covering her completely. "No bigger than my hand when she was born."

"How did she eat?"

"Infants usually eat their mother's food, much like your own breastmilk, but her gul father had to feed her." Quaint closed his eyes. "If he could, he would have given her the food from his mouth, like birds do, if that had made her live just a little longer . . ."

Ariadne understood, turning around, the tip of her finger brushing against the ring with the braid. The retroreflector layer of tissue behind his retina had a greenish tinge, and it should have scared her, but didn't, and she brought him to her chest. *Let's talk about this later*, his expression seemed to say, and Ariadne had no dreams in the few hours she spent in bed. It reminded her of the day she woke up in Erik's house for the first time, her mind floating aimlessly in an endless darkness, and only a vague command keeping her from going astray: *follow the thread, Ariadne, follow the thread.*

When she opened her eyes, she realized that Quaint was gone, and there were people talking in the living room of the suite.

"Can't you just call her?"

"She needs to sleep. The night was long enough."

"I'm pretty sure we're all banned from Cabaré after this, anyway . . ."

Blinking, Ariadne recognized the voices. Quaint, calm and stable; Rafaela, a little nervous but not aggressive; Augusto, finishing with an ironic chuckle. She staggered to her feet and entered the bathroom to take a fast shower. Her left arm had deep holes where Damião had bitten her, and she was sometimes assaulted by glitches of feeling, but most of the sensors had been shattered by the bite.

I should have bought a condom, she thought blankly, remembering what they had talked about and watching as the water ran down the drain. Sometimes, she could still feel the taste of the pill Minotauro used to give her dissolving under her tongue, but she pushed the thought away.

Ariadne put the dress on again and opened the door, and the three guls turned around to see her. Quaint was on the other seat of the sofa, with a cigarette between his fingers, the living room smelling strongly of smoke.

"What is this, the after party?" Ariadne took the cigarette from his hand and put it out on a tray. *I thought you were stopping*, she mouthed, and Quaint smiled: *I guess I overestimated myself.*

"Rafaela harassed me until I agreed to bring her here," explained Augusto with a tired hand wave. He was still wearing his tuxedo, or part of it: the midnight-blue jacket was missing, the white shirt had brown bloodstains and the sleeves had been rolled up, the tie was crooked, and the shoes were caked with mud.

The other woman opened her mouth to speak, then lowered her head. Rafaela had managed to change from her evening gown into a casual jumpsuit, but she had lines of mascara streaking her cheeks, her hair tied into a lousy ponytail. Ariadne felt a wicked satisfaction in knowing she had not been the only one crying, but she kept her expression unreadable.

"Were you telling the truth?" asked Rafaela with a faltering voice. "That you would help me no matter what?"

"Yes, I was."

"*Help?*" Quaint's eye was white and glassy, but he could

already open it. Ariadne took one of the bags from the drugstore and knelt on the sofa as she spoke, cleaning his face and applying another disposable patch onto his eye.

"She'll take us to Erik in exchange for medical help." Ariadne brushed the hair from his brow. "Right, Rafaela?"

"Right," Rafaela answered bitterly. "And Damião . . ."

"He'll wake up in a few days, but that doesn't matter, does it? Sacrifices must be made for our agreement."

"So you knew where Erik was all along." Quaint was also far from his meticulous self, although he didn't look as battered as the night before. He wore only the burgundy pants and his hair was down, but his skin had regained some of its color after the blood loss and his voice was stronger. "Care to tell us what is going on?"

Rafaela turned on the television. The anchorwoman spoke for her:

> *". . . analyzing the last footage of the president, we can see him from the window of his house in the rural area of Rio de Janeiro, accompanied by a nurse. When contacted, she refused to speak to our reporters, and . . ."*

"I bet Quaint can imagine why they were searching for Erik," said Rafaela. "Why he would perform a botched gulification on the goddamn president is what *I* want to know."

His shoulder blades stiffened. "He promised me he wouldn't do it."

Augusto clicked his tongue. "Can we trust Erik's word?"

"Keep going, Rafaela," said Ariadne.

"I talked to Erik on the phone before they went to the club. I knew when they would come for him because Lena told me, and that made him decide to hide in Genebra's house. I helped . . . for a price." Rafaela chewed the corner of her thumb. "He never paid me back."

"Friedrich once said that the president had terminal cancer and they were covering it up," said Augusto. "I thought they wanted Erik to do something about it."

"The same thing he did with himself, but Erik refused, and I needed him around because of the pregnancy." A cynical smile appeared on Rafaela's wide lips. "At first, he promised he would think about it, then he started to ignore my letters. Said he didn't feel comfortable."

"Then you ratted him out." Augusto sighed. "Why did they take Genebra?"

Quaint pressed his ring, and his fingertips became white. "Because he needs a living gul to do it. What about the eaten advisers?"

The pregnant gul smirked. "Genebra needs to eat."

"More importantly, where are they?" asked Ariadne.

According to Rafaela, Erik and Genebra were being kept in a house in Petrópolis, a historical town in the Fluminense Mountains. *If we leave now, we can arrive in an hour or two*, the gul said, caressing her belly distractedly. *But only after curfew.* Quaint and Ariadne exchanged a look. *I say we all go*, suggested Augusto. *I'm worried about Genebra, and if I'm there, it's three against one.*

After another hour discussing the plan, they agreed to leave at ten. Rafaela and Augusto waited in the reception area as they dressed and made the final preparations, and Quaint closed the door behind them.

"I haven't been completely honest about Erik."

"I'm listening," said Ariadne, leaving her purse next to a pile of journals. Since the others had left, she had acted as clinically as possible, finding everything she would need, changing clothes, charging her phone and limbs. Quaint grabbed one of the leather notebooks and leafed through the pages.

The journal he had in his hands was the same one she had been reading, and a small note fell from inside of it.

Maybe we will love each other better in another life, Erik had written. *If we don't, and we're always like this, in this constant cycle of affection and disdain, I hope we can at least remain—as we always have been, in this and other lives—the greatest of friends.*

"What is your opinion of him right now?"

"It's hard to say." Ariadne put the note back, keeping it safe between two pages. "I don't know how to reconcile the things he did to you with the man who took care of me. I feel like I should be grateful that he even believed me worthy of living, or I won't deserve these limbs." She opened and closed her hand, looking at the fine machinery of the fingers without the synthetic skin. "At the same time, I don't want to make little of your pain."

"Then we feel the same." Except for the eye patch, Quaint looked just like he did on the day they met: hair slicked back, mustard-yellow shirt, suspenders, pants, brogues. He took an extra pair of glasses from his suitcase, and his eyes were hidden again. "Erik and I were romantically involved from 1949 to 1971. I didn't know how to tell you before, mostly because I don't like to think of it myself. It's shameful to admit that someone hurt you so profoundly, and you still care about their well-being."

"I know." Ariadne pointed at the journal. "I read it."

"I was afraid that you had," admitted Quaint. "I don't know what kind of things he wrote about me. The little I've seen . . . That's not how I wanted you to get to know me."

"I learned nothing about you from his journals. I learned only what another person *thought* of you at a moment in time. Only you can show me if his conclusions are true or not."

Quaint smiled with relief. "I am grateful."

"No need to be. Whoever you loved . . . To me, right now, I only care if you still do."

"Only with the fond bitterness reserved for those we have known for the longest. I did not lie when we met. Nowadays, Erik is my friend," said Quaint, taking his card to unlock the door. "A friend I would like very much to punch in the face, but a friend nonetheless."

Raindrops clashed against the window of the rented car. It was dark outside, but every time the police stopped them, the guls showed their membership cards, and the cops let them go without a question. In Rio, creatures moved in alleyways, and death squads patrolled the avenues as they passed. *If they stop us one more time, I'll eat them*, Augusto muttered between his teeth, and Rafaela let out a pleased chortle.

Ariadne clutched one of Erik's journals. Reading them was the only comfort she had left now; the only tie to him, no matter how faint, the only reminder that he was a person she'd once met and could soon find again. She also wanted a connection—any connection—between the Erik she knew and the one Quaint knew, a unifying factor between two seemingly opposing forces: his Erik, her Erik, and the real Erik, who belonged only to himself. By her side, Quaint was a statue, eyes closed and spine straight, resting again as his regeneration process continued. She glanced at the notebook, the date on the cover corresponding to one of the years Erik had spent with her:

> *Today I woke up feeling like I could breathe again. It's strange, because I have in fact been breathing all this time, in the sense that, when I inhale, my diaphragm contracts and my lungs expand, enlarging my chest cavity. But merely breathing has not been enough, it seems. What I mean is: I think I'm quite happy with this life.*

Erik wrote in another entry: *Sometimes, she behaves like a mean cat. I say that because there are no mean cats in reality, like there are no mean dogs: animals are reactive, not evil. Case in point: Ariadne insulted me a few times and retreated to her room, but at night surprised me with a plate of blini. How did she learn? She didn't say. She just said she didn't want me to miss home.*

The car was silent except for the news and the sound of the rain. Augusto lowered the volume of the radio when he realized the other two guls were napping or pretending to, and Ariadne kept reading with the light of her cell phone.

> *During any recovery period, we know that there are days that are rougher than others, but that doesn't make any of them less difficult. Today has been one of those days. Ariadne made a sexual advance toward me, and I can't say I hadn't realized that it would happen at some point. I just pretended not to notice her interest. Acknowledging it made me feel like an old man trying to flatter himself, but it was there, and I don't know what to make of it.*

Erik left the rest of the page blank, then continued on another day: *A. is too ashamed to leave her bedroom now, and I know I broke her heart. Please, I tried to tell her through the door, please understand I am not disgusted by you in any way. You're just too young. My heart is worried, saddened, filled with compassion. Whatever I lost that day with the rope around my neck only returned with you.*

Her damaged hand twitched, and Ariadne put the notebook aside. Augusto met her eyes in the rearview mirror.

"Awake?"

"Can't sleep at a time like this."

"That's wise of you," answered Augusto with a smile. "Are you hungry? I underestimated how much gas we were going to need. I can get you something while we fill the tank."

"I am, actually. Thank you for asking."

Augusto stopped at a gas station in the middle of the empty road, and she followed him into the convenience store. The only person present was the attendant, and the woman lowered her head, avoiding their faces, like she knew what they were.

"I've been thinking about our last conversation," said Augusto as she chose a bottle of water and a protein bar. "About purpose and ethics."

"Your purpose is existing." Ariadne unwrapped the bar and took a bite, eyeing the clerk as she filled the tank of the car. "Every living being is part of a lineage of creatures that yearn to keep existing. Guls are no different."

"That's what got me thinking." Behind Augusto, the muted television showed footage of protests in multiple cities, demanding the end of curfew. "I understand we exist, and to keep existing, we have to eat. Yet here we are. You and I. Talking. Working together. Because we *can* do it. How to reconcile the fact that we were made in each other's likeness, but I have to kill my equals to stay alive?"

"It feels like you're asking me to justify why you should

die, or why I deserve to." Ariadne considered him. Augusto was not much taller than her, but he still felt bigger with his wide torso, strong arms, thick neck. "And I won't."

"What I mean is that I do see a purpose now. Maybe not concrete. But when I look at this . . ." Augusto pointed at the television, then at the car. "You know, Ariadne, every gul I have ever met was born inside a palace."

"A palace?"

"My parents served the Mwene of Mutapa when I was a child. My father came from Great Zimbabwe, my mother from the Manden. Although she was more of a diplomat, she fought alongside the Lion of Mali in the Battle of Kirina, and served Mansa Musa. It's what guls have done since the dawn of time: sided with the powerful to fill their bellies, and the humans have used our strength for political gain. Did Quaint tell you about his parents?"

"No."

"They're the same as mine. His father presented himself as a scholar but served six different dynasties. His mother arrived at court with the Yuan and was infamously vicious against those who defied the emperors. She betrayed the Yuan for the Ming, then the Ming for the Qing, and would have betrayed them, too, if she had not retired to grieve for his father by the time of the revolution." Augusto opened his wallet and counted bills. "Quaint grew up in the Forbidden City, surrounded by palace women and government officials. Just like all of us did."

"Rafaela, too, I suppose."

"Oh, yes. I don't know where her father came from, but her mother was good friends with most of the Braganzas. Rafaela came with the Portuguese to Brazil during the Napoleonic Wars. In the *Príncipe Real*, no less," added Augusto. "Genebra, too, but she was born under the House of

Burgundy. She was so used to life in court that she never hunted in her life. I could list other guls for hours."

Ariadne hugged herself when they went outside, shivering with the breeze.

"Are you thinking about this because of the government officials who are after Erik?"

"The president, Erik, the news. Our purpose . . . It might be pointless. It might be cruel that we even exist, for both sides. Maybe this is the wrong word. Purpose implies design," said Augusto. "I decided that if I have to take, I will give as well. This is why I'm here. If guls helped establish this political chaos, we should help dismantle it."

They stopped speaking when the clerk finished bagging their purchases, and Ariadne rubbed his arm with more affection than she expected while he paid for everything. The others were already awake inside the car. Rafaela looked awfully bored as she removed her fake nails with acetone and tweezers from her handbag, and Quaint looked at the dark forest lining the road.

"We're close now," said Rafaela when they locked the doors. "Can you smell it?"

Quaint interlaced his fingers with Ariadne's.

"When we arrive, you need to promise me you will stay by my side at all times," he told her in a low voice.

"I promise."

"I can also protect you!" argued Rafaela, looking at them through the rearview mirror. She touched her belly over her striped jumpsuit and flashed a malicious grin. "You don't know how hungry this girl makes me."

"My mother says it's like having a parasite inside you." Quaint caressed the back of Ariadne's hand with his thumb distractedly, but she could see the anxiety in his posture.

"Mine said it was the best three years of her life." Augusto had his eyes focused on the road. "To each their own."

"It's a little bit of both!" Rafaela gestured, her real fingernails looking dry and brittle without the polished extensions. "In any case, I hope the house is full of people. Security. Assistants. That sort of thing. They don't exaggerate when they say pregnant women even eat other guls . . ."

Augusto clicked his tongue. "That's the kind of unnecessary information we don't want to know when we're all stuck inside a car with you, Rafaela."

"I'm sorry, I'm full of energy!" The other woman turned around to wink at Ariadne, white teeth against tawny skin. "See? I'll protect you."

"Don't overdo it, Rafaela," replied Ariadne. "You'll burst a vein."

"You already ruined my social life." Rafaela laughed like they had not fought twenty-four hours ago. "Might as well stick to you."

The car stopped in front of a vast plot located on a hill next to Petrópolis. There was a farm in the background, a small hut, and a guardhouse outside the gate. All the other houses were one or more kilometers away, and the only sound came from the orchestra of crickets and frogs hidden in the grass. The rain had already stopped, but Ariadne couldn't see much of the place besides the full moon and the distant lights of the farm.

"Come with me, Augusto." Rafaela unlocked the door. She removed her high heels and walked barefoot on the grass, curls escaping from her low ponytail. "I'm starving and I need to find a guard."

"Goodness, woman . . ."

Quaint waited until they were alone to face her. He seemed to have considered his words carefully when he spoke with a grave tone:

"I could have forgiven Erik for the gulification if it was just pettiness, you see." The light of the car was reflected in his glasses, and the shadow of the leaves wandered across the skin of his face. "But he knew what the implications meant to me. He said it could help hybrid children, but it was just an exercise in curiosity."

Ariadne touched the ring with the braid without a word, and he continued:

"I thought Fanny wouldn't make it. The pregnancy took thirteen months, dangerously short for a gul, tortuously long for a human." Quaint lowered his head. "My mother and I fed her with our own blood, but Fanny was forty when she delivered, and it took an enormous toll on her health."

"But your daughter didn't make it."

"Mochou lived less than twenty years." Quaint accepted her arms around him, bringing him closer to her chest to cradle him. "First, she couldn't hold things anymore. She could hardly write as we were teaching her because her little hands trembled. She couldn't walk. She cried and laughed at inappropriate times. Still, the gul in her kept her alive, suffering, struggling, but alive. And I could do nothing to make it better or release Mochou from the pain. Nothing, my little girl . . ."

"I'm sorry," murmured Ariadne. "I'm sorry."

Quaint remained like that for a moment, breathing in the closeness, clutching her arm around himself. Then, he straightened his back, staring at the window.

"It's been more than a hundred years, but the love for a child keeps hurting still. Erik . . ."

A piercing scream interrupted whatever he'd meant to say.

Quaint reacted immediately, reversing their positions to cover her face and ears. Another scream, and Ariadne shut her eyes, trying to focus on the beating of his heart, on the soothing hum coming from her own throat. She didn't even know which song it was, she just needed something—anything—to block the sound. After a short, unnerving silence, the screams were replaced by an animal roar, like that of a large feline, or the hiss of a threatened snake, and Quaint held her even tighter.

Then there was only silence.

"We should go," he said gently, and Ariadne nodded in agreement.

Augusto and Rafaela were nowhere to be seen. The gates were open, the air still, and a vague realization crossed her mind: *they don't want me to see the bodies.* Quaint left his glasses in the breast pocket of his shirt and removed the eye patch.

"I'm quite sensitive to the light, but I was gifted with exceptional night vision," said Quaint, bending forward. "Stay behind me, Ariadne."

Meters ahead, a man opened the front door of the farmhouse. Quaint stretched his neck and roared, the sound bubbling from his chest upward. Ariadne hid behind him, feeling his body vibrating, remembering Erik's old lessons: *a larger larynx with lengthened vocal cords, capable of producing a potent roar, with great resonance . . .*

The man shot first. The bullet hit a trunk, far from where they were, and Quaint bared his fangs. His upper lip curled, propelling his teeth forward, and even his incisors, the most humanlike teeth a gul could have, were a warning sign: teeth that could break bone and capture prey, holding it still for the canines to slice. Quaint dashed toward the stranger, who threw the gun on the grass, covering his face with his remaining limb.

"I'm unarmed! Please—*please*!"

The human cowered on the ground. Quaint stepped on the gun, cracking the barrel, and took the phone from the pocket of the man's jacket, crushing it with his hand, pieces of silicon, plastic, and aluminum running through his fingers like breadcrumbs. His eyes reflected the light that came from the house, glowing in the dark.

Like tigers, they can move fast, but only in short bursts, Erik had said with a knowing smile. Quaint kept the human on the ground, his shoe on his back. *Most break the spinal cord by crushing the windpipe before eating. Their hands are so strong that they can smash a skull with the pressure. Fascinating stuff, right?*

"We're the only ones here . . ." The man trembled like he had never seen a gul. "Only us and the doctor."

"Erik Yurkov?" Ariadne placed a hand on Quaint's sleeve when he lifted the man by the collar of his shirt, a quiet warning that he shouldn't overdo it. The man nodded frenetically.

"With the president." He pointed at the stairs, and a high-pitched sob escaped his lips. "The Russian is upstairs with the president."

Quaint put him back on the ground, and the man fell to his knees.

"Stay quiet and don't do anything you will regret," Quaint warned, colder than she had ever heard him sound. "The others are hungry."

The house was deserted. The lights were all on, and the television in the living room aired a foreign movie, but there was no one on the couches, chairs, or armchairs. The kitchen was empty except for a whistling kettle, and everything smelled sterile, like the walls had been repeatedly washed with bleach. Quaint turned off the stove before proceeding to the stairway, and Ariadne followed him upstairs.

The second floor was the same. A long corridor with multiple rooms, made eerie by its unending silence, shadows flickering like creeping ghosts. Quaint opened the first door—nothing. They had the same result with the second and third doors, until they reached one that was locked. *Stay back*, he mouthed, pressing his palm against the door until it fell down.

An emaciated middle-aged woman was sitting in a straw rocking chair. She had crow's feet all around her eyes; her brown hair was streaked with gray strands in a short, lifeless bob; her hooked nose covered half of her oval face. Ariadne recognized her immediately as Genebra.

"Quaint, dear, we knew you would come." Genebra tried to maintain a graceful expression, but as soon as she spoke, her voice broke and tears flowed freely down her cheeks. Quaint pulled her into a hug, brushing her dry hair with his fingers as if she were a frail crystal figurine. "I couldn't take it any longer."

There was nothing suspicious in the bedroom, just a bed in disarray, a clothes rack with a few dresses, and a simple vanity with jewelry similar to what Ariadne had seen in Genebra's house. Nothing except the thick chain that hung from a hook on the wall and went to Genebra's right ankle. Quaint took the iron in his hands, snapping it.

"You look so thin." Quaint caressed Genebra's head. "Are they feeding you?"

"Only every two or three months, just an arm and a leg . . ." She lifted her chin to face him, tears streaking her pale cheeks. Her eyes had sunk into hollow pits with the weight loss. "Soon, there won't be any more assistants . . ."

"Did anybody hurt you?"

"No—I'm just the guinea pig. Erik . . ."

"Did he use you? For the gulification?"

Genebra hurried to speak; her voice slurred like she had been drugged and her eyes looked dilated and unfocused. "It's not his fault—I swear, Erik only . . ."

Quaint's expression shifted to the same coldness she had seen in him outside.

"You're going home today," Quaint assured her. Ariadne was already in the corridor, their conversation sounding more and more distant. "I promise."

A muffled noise could be heard from behind the last door, something wild and anguished, like a long, hollow moan. She touched the doorknob, and the door opened on its own, revealing the last room.

The place was illuminated only by a lamp. There was an elderly man tied to a stretcher, his body twisted in unnatural angles with an empty blood bag connected to his arm by a catheter, a black blotch spreading on the skin around the tube. Ariadne was paralyzed by the sight, an invisible hand invading her stomach, piercing organs and pulling entrails. The man's mouth was gagged with a cloth, probably to prevent him from screaming as he flailed until he broke both arms, rejecting the gul màterial.

First, the vision reminded her of herself—wriggling, body bent into uncomfortable angles—then it reminded her of . . . No, no, she couldn't think of them. Ariadne forced herself to glance at the man; his face was familiar, like the images repeated on the news . . .

"Ariadne?" Somebody called her, but it wasn't Quaint. His voice was softer, his accent thicker; the pronunciation of her name sounded different coming from his lips. It wasn't Quaint, but he held her nonetheless, pulling her to his chest and covering her eyes like she was still the stupid, broken teenager he'd once met.

Ariadne squirmed inside his arms, but he was taller, stronger, unwilling to let go. Erik kept her in a firm hug, tightening his grip when she tried to escape.

"Let me go—" Ariadne clawed Erik's hand, ungrasping his fingers, her feet thrashing in the air. *Don't touch me*, she thought, alarmed and unreasonable. She would scratch if she had nails made of keratin, so she did what she could, biting his arm, elbowing his chest. Her feet didn't even reach the floor, but she wanted to hurt him somehow. "Let me go, let me go!"

"Darling, darling, you shouldn't see this kind of thing." Erik's voice was gentle, but he continued to try to drag her back to the door. In her head, all she could see was the yellow house, her feet hitting the stairs as Minotauro pulled her by the neck, one, two, three, four, scattering bruises on her old skin.

Ariadne sank her teeth into his hand, trying to show that she wanted to decide for herself if she could take it or not, hoping to rip the soft flesh. Erik let out a groan.

"Let her go."

They stopped moving. This time, the voice belonged to Quaint, and there was no difference between the way he spoke to the amputated man downstairs and the way he spoke to Erik. Erik did not obey. He continued to cover her eyes, but the quick instant of recognition allowed her to slither out of his grasp to run to Quaint.

"Hello, old friend." Erik smiled behind an uncharacteristic

stubble. Then he walked to the body and covered the stretcher with a sheet. "I knew you would come, but you shouldn't have brought her with you, no matter how persuasive she can be. And Ariadne, my good, good girl—it's not healthy for you to see this kind of thing."

This kind of thing. The words echoed in her mind. That kind of thing, like the children in the surgery room; that kind of thing, her own limbs, or what was left of them; that kind of thing, waking up and finding there was nothing of Erik left. Ariadne blew out the air she was holding, feeling like Quaint's anger was contagious, or maybe it had been her anger all along, hidden in a little box inside her year after year, coming undone.

"What wasn't good for me was being left behind! Asking the neighbors if they saw you, and being told you left through the front door with suitcases under your arms. *That* was not good for me!" Ariadne knew she was yelling, and her cheeks burned with shame. She could only see Erik's back while he petted the unconscious man's head comfortingly. "You even went back to the clinic to store your damn journals—you went back without telling me—and you did this, all of this, you . . ."

Erik took off his gloves. His lab coat was dirty, his hair more silver than blond, his mouth dry and split.

"You're right. I'm deeply sorry for all the harm I caused." He smiled in that way that Ariadne remembered, generous and sweet, scratching his own nape like he'd gotten caught stealing from the cookie jar. "I never learn, do I?"

"You're shameless, that's what you are." Quaint ground his teeth, and a guttural sound came from his throat. "Everyone else is just a pawn to you."

"I suppose I should apologize to you as well," admitted

Erik with a thoughtful tone. "I always involve you in my mess, don't I?"

Quaint roared, and in a second he was in front of Erik, seizing him by the throat.

"You promised me you would never do it again. I *trusted* you."

"Quaint!" Ariadne ran to hug Quaint from behind. "Please, calm down, please, I beg—"

"I can't calm down," muttered Quaint, squeezing Erik's neck. Ariadne tightened the hug, her cheek against his spine and her hands pulling down his arms to make him stop hurting Erik. "He *caused* all of this."

"I know I betrayed your trust in the past." Erik attempted to touch his shoulder. "I know I had no right, but I swear . . ."

Quaint would have growled again, but he stopped when he saw Ariadne's hands had fallen from their grasp, weakened by the effort. He turned around to face her, and all his fury dissipated when he realized she was scared, lonely, trembling. Both men were quiet for a few moments, and Quaint looked down, a lock of hair falling on his forehead. He held her two bionic hands as if her fingers could break if they were not touched with the utmost care.

Thank you, he mouthed, his voice barely a whisper. *I'm calmer now.*

"Quaint, he didn't have a choice." Genebra leaned against the wall and stumbled as she walked. "They kept us here to force us to do it. It didn't work. The president will die at any moment."

"Both of you can give as many excuses as you like. Nothing will change the fact that he started this to have a few extra years of life to keep studying." Quaint's laughter was sharp and mirthless, almost a bark. "None of us would be here right now if Erik had done the right thing in the past. Do you regret it, at least?"

Erik glanced at the man under the sheet.

"I regret this situation. I regret having used you for my research. I was cruel, angry, and unfair when I did that to you, and I should have asked before deciding on my own." He paused briefly, then looked at Ariadne, pressing his lips in a weak smile. *That* smile, the smile he showed exclusively to her. "I don't regret what I accomplished with the borrowed decades."

Ariadne stepped forward and offered her numbed hand to Erik.

"Erik, we need to leave."

"I don't know if that's a good idea," said Erik. "The squad will come back in the morning to make sure we're still here."

"The guls won't let them near you anymore. You can come back."

Erik touched her face, the tips of his calloused fingers drawing circles on her cheek.

"You grew up."

"Time passes for everyone." Ariadne pulled him by the arm, avoiding his gaze. "Let's go home."

Quaint helped Genebra down the stairs, Erik took their belongings to the first floor, and Ariadne found herself alone in the empty corridor. When she lifted her face, Rafaela was there, illuminated by one of the fluorescent lights. Her bare feet were soiled with mud, her long curls covered her long face, and she had dark red stains on her light clothes.

"It all comes to an end," Rafaela said in a singsong voice, but the feral intonation of her roar still crept into her words. "After this, we're free from this part of the deal."

"I guess we are." Ariadne covered her nose with her hand.

The stench of death was growing stronger, and she looked the other way.

"I can smell the blood for miles, you know," said Rafaela. Her smile looked like a snarl as she walked past Ariadne, bumping against her numb arm. "Wait for me in the car."

Epilogue

In Vitória, in a three-story building located in Rua da Encruzilhada, there was an inconspicuous clinic, frequented only by a discreet group of longevous patients. Guls of the entire country came to find the only two humans who could look after their health. Ariadne had missed her home; it was not as luxurious as the hotel, or as refined as Cabaré, but the peace she found there was not easy to replace.

She yawned, curled up in bed. Quaint lay behind her, one arm wrapped around her small frame to cup her breast, his heavy jaw resting comfortably in the curve of her neck.

"Good morning," murmured Ariadne, removing the charger from her limbs and turning around to see him. Quaint rolled over to lie on his back, head against the bedpost, and looked lazily at the hour on his phone. "Any news?"

"Nothing interesting. My mother called, but I managed to avoid speaking since you were still asleep and I would find it extremely distasteful to remove my arm and risk waking you up." Quaint offered a grin. "Genebra asked if we want to spend a weekend in Rio. She wants to thank you. Augusto also messaged me, letting us know that I have not been banned from Cabaré—sad news—and you have been formally invited to attend again, if you wish. It seems you have made an impression."

"They can keep the impression to themselves." Ariadne crawled over him to find her bra, but he grabbed her legs so she could sit on his lap.

"Just a little longer, Doctor."

Ariadne smiled, her cynicism vanishing with the request. "You're getting spoiled."

"What can I do? You make me weak."

The trip to Rio had been silent, all of them squeezed inside Erik's yellow Jeep. *I can take off my legs*, Ariadne had suggested lightly, which seemed to horrify everyone but Erik. *Ariadne*, Quaint had said, and she smiled, ignoring the blood and the hurt. *I really can.* He insisted on returning with them, at least for the first week. *Neither of them are to be trusted*, he had said, and she thought of arguing that it would not be in Rafaela's best interests to hurt her; besides, she wasn't afraid of a centennial, academic old man. But she said nothing. After the first week passed, Vitória Airport closed for a day due to poor weather, and she suggested that he stay for another week. *It would help me a lot*, Ariadne had commented. *Rafaela is a handful.*

Each day, they would either ignore the subject or find another equally poor excuse. *The tickets are expensive today*, she said over his shoulder as he scrolled through the airline's website, and he nodded in agreement. Quaint also brought up that the cat had taken a liking to sleeping by his side in bed, and the fact that she had more patients now that the guls of Cabaré knew who she was; *yes, it would be safe to have you around*, she conceded.

"When are you planning to come back?" The question came without warning, even to herself. "I was thinking we should start investigating what's happening to your tattoos."

Quaint seemed surprised. "I almost forgot about it."

"But you would have to stay a little longer . . ."

"About that—" He opened his mouth to speak, then closed it again, tongue against his front teeth under the lip.

"Yes?"

"Investigating sounds wonderful."

Ariadne kissed him and hopped off the bed. She hooked her bra and tried to find the rest of her clothes amid the mess they'd left on the chair the night before. She ended up wearing his mustard shirt, rolling the sleeves up to her elbows, the length of it reaching the middle of her thighs. Quaint stayed in bed, watching her with a smile on his face.

"Mr. Boniface will arrive soon," said Ariadne, pulling away the sheets that covered him to force him to get up. "He still can't understand that I need to have lunch every day."

"A very serious issue. That and his growing hypochondria." Quaint snickered, putting on his undershirt. "I can watch you eat after you're finished."

"I'd like to, if the others don't bother us to death."

Ariadne left the main bedroom and stared at Erik's office at the end of the corridor. He had been inside of it most of the time since they arrived, appearing only sometimes to eat with her. During the day, he locked himself in the office and Ariadne could hear furniture being moved around, books relocated from their shelves, and objects packed into boxes. Quaint mostly ignored the other two, with the exception of the times he and Erik went to the rooftop to smoke, or when Rafaela had real pregnancy needs, not just whims and complaints.

Erik also avoided interrupting them; maybe he was ashamed of what he'd done and wanted to respect their time. Or maybe it was the same as always, and he was too caught up in his world of ideas, incapable of letting anyone else in.

Ariadne knocked on the door.

After a few seconds, Erik stuck out his head, sandy hair disheveled, shirt crumpled, but at least he was shaving again. She did her best to hide her smile when she saw the disaster behind him. Erik seemed to read her thoughts and looked down at his mismatched socks, laughing as well.

"I really am a bumbling fool," Erik said, opening the door and hurrying to find her a chair amid the piles of books. "Please don't mind my chaos. I was trying to find out if there was anything useful in my old things."

"It's all yours." Ariadne peeked around at the rest of the office. There were two closed suitcases in the corner, and the desk was a mess. "Is that another prosthesis?"

"Ah! The arm! Yes, yes, wait a second . . ." Erik went to the other side of the desk, his lanky legs avoiding the objects on the floor. He grabbed a limp left arm and took it to Ariadne. "It was about time that I made you new ones. And now that your arm is damaged . . ."

Ariadne stretched her arm toward him, and Erik held her by the hand, her fingertips between his index and middle fingers, his thumb pulling slowly to reveal the limb underneath. He rolled down the skin above her elbow, looking with awe at the limb he had built for her. The joints and articulations, the delicate structure engineered to imitate human shape, the lightweight material, the dots indicating each sensor. Erik compared the two prostheses, stretching Ariadne's arm to calculate each of their lengths, measuring them like doll parts.

"I think you're a little taller."

"Not much. Not compared to you."

"You can't compare yourself to me, of all people!" Erik let

out a hearty laugh, pulling out a little stool to sit by her side. He'd always had horrible posture, and had changed nothing, bending forward so they were eye to eye. "The average height in Russia is different from the one in Brazil, and if we consider sexual dimorphism, genetic background, and . . ."

"No, you three are giants. At least Ms. Terebê is shorter than me." Ariadne glanced again at the suitcases, and her shoulders felt heavy, as if all the strength she had mustered in the past months was gone. "Are you leaving?"

Erik set the prosthesis on his lap, playing with its fingers. "Well . . . I . . ."

"Yes or no? I'm not trying to stop you."

"I think it's the best thing I can do." Erik attempted a smile, but failed when he saw the glacial expression on Ariadne's face. "I have caused enough harm. And now that I know that you're well, despite everything, and that you're not alone . . ."

"You're not bothering *me*."

"But I'm too ashamed to look at you, Ariadne. And Quaint, too." Erik ran his fingers through his hair. Now she could see that he had aged in the last few years, not as much as he should have, but enough to create more lines in his thin face, and for the silvery strands to cover most of his head. Still, he was the same Erik who had held her so tenderly in her worst moments, the same Erik who had abandoned her. "I mess up time and time again. I'm unable to maintain any relationship."

"You are, that much is true. But you also have to admit that you hate feeling stuck." Ariadne intertwined her fingers with the prosthesis he was holding, the new one perfect and brilliant compared to her old hand. "After you were done with me, you had to find a new project to work on. You only stopped when they found you."

"It's the only thing I know how to do. Studying, inventing. I was never good with people. If I were, I would never have left you behind. I would have never walked out the door without saying goodbye."

"You could have taken me with you," Ariadne said softly. "I would have gone."

Erik looked at her. It was not pity, what she found in the grayish-blue of his eyes, but something she could not yet discern.

"I know you would, and that's why I didn't. You need stability, and I don't deserve such touching devotion." Erik took her hand again to dress her with the skin, first slipping her fingers, tucking them under the fake nails, then straightening the skin of her arm. "But I guess the stars have aligned. Quaint is the people person, not me. The one who knows how to say the right thing, who can understand what others mean even when they don't say it."

"Don't blame Quaint because you prioritize your curiosity above us." Ariadne flicked his nose with a finger. "Anyway. Whatever you choose to do with your life is your problem, not mine."

Erik squeezed her hand again like he wanted to hold her for longer, his bony fingers covering hers, the pink tinge of his skin visible against her yellowness, the sun freckles and veins giving away his age.

"Quaint is a good man," Erik finally said. "I'm sure he'll take proper care of you."

"I *know* he's a good man," replied Ariadne. "You think I would let him stay if I didn't trust him?"

Erik chuckled. "Oh, that much is true. You were always suspicious. A mean little cat."

Ariadne stood up, dusting the mustard shirt. "I think the new arm is too light, by the way."

"You think?" Erik weighed the limb again, his voice growing more energetic. "I can fix it."

"Only after lunch. Mr. Boni will arrive in no time," she said, pulling Erik by the collar of his shirt to lead him into the corridor. "It's your turn to cook. Rafaela and Quaint are constantly forcing me to try fancy silly takeout to see what the dishes look like, and I'm tired of it."

Erik laughed as he followed her down the stairs. Quaint was already there, sitting on the armchair with the white cat sleeping on his lap. Rafaela lay on the sofa, her legs over two pillows, while her cell phone buzzed on the coffee table.

"It's just Damião," she said, sucking on a blood bag. "I told him I won't come back, but he's a slow learner."

"You're just torturing him now."

Damião had been calling nonstop since he woke up alone in their house, and Rafaela took joy in alternating between ignoring and insulting him. *I thought you'd be grieving this relationship*, Ariadne had told her a few days before, eyebrows raised in disbelief. *I am, I am an absolute wreck!* Rafaela had argued back while Ariadne did her pedicure at her request, not sounding like an absolute wreck at all. *I have cried myself to exhaustion, but whenever he cries back, I feel* so *much better . . .*

"Well, if he's not doing anything dangerous, I don't care."

. . . The Federal Police continue to investigate the connection between the militia known popularly as death squads . . . read the chyron on the television screen, as the anchorwoman spoke: *"The funeral will be held tomorrow with a closed casket. After going missing for twelve days, the president's death was confirmed on Monday, while . . ."*

Ariadne didn't know what would happen next. If Quaint would stay, if Rafaela would keep her promise, if Erik would disappear within a week or remain at the clinic forever. It didn't matter; she was happy—she craved, *desired* happiness—maybe for the very first time.

The intercom rang, and the cat lifted her head. Ariadne walked past them, checked the camera, and pressed the button that unlocked the entrance.

ACKNOWLEDGMENTS

A considerably shorter version of *Cabaret in Flames* was published in Brazilian Portuguese by Mafagafo Revista, and I'm thankful both to its editors, Jana Bianchi and Fernanda Castro, and to the readers who were excited about it, but thought it should have been longer. I obviously agree, and hope this one delivers!

As for the English editions, I have to thank my agent, Lee O'Brien, and the teams at Tor and Titan. In the US: Sanaa Ali-Virani; Jennifer Gunnels and her assistant, Julianna Kim; Christine Foltzer; and Kat Howard. In the UK: Daniel Carpenter and Charlotte Kelly. The artists behind the two lovely covers, Zoë van Dijk and Natasha MacKenzie, also have my gratitude, as do all the copyeditors.

On a more personal note:

Juliana, who was one of the first people to read the story and offered additional support and color counseling.

Dante, every (or almost every) love interest I write has something of you. Quaint is no different.

And finally, acknowledging in the sense of recognizing, not thanking, this story wouldn't have taken the shape it did if it weren't for my own life. Without the man who constantly threatened to do to me what was done to her if I ever got away, Ariadne would not exist. You were just a small thread in the patchwork of memories and people that turned into Minotauro, one of many, really, but this specific idea belongs to you, not to me.

ABOUT THE AUTHOR

Hache Pueyo is an Argentine-Brazilian writer and translator. She is the author of the novella *But Not Too Bold* and the bilingual collection *A Study in Ugliness & Outras Histórias*. She won an Otherwise Fellowship for her work with gender in speculative fiction, and her work has appeared as H. Pueyo in *The Magazine of Fantasy & Science Fiction, Clarkesworld, Strange Horizons,* and *The Year's Best Dark Fantasy & Horror,* among others.

hachepueyo.com
Instagram: @hachepueyo
Bluesky: @hachepueyo.bsky.social